"Can you take a picture of me and Tess jumping up and down and yelling?"

My mom's eyebrow went up, but only a little bit, which is just fine. It's the way she asks "Why?" without having to say it out loud.

"I want to include it in my letter to the dictionary people," I said.

"What word are you suggesting this time?"

"*Vexylent*," I said. "I just came up with it yesterday. It's short for 'very, extremely excellent,' and I think having a picture of how it feels will help."

"I'm sure it wouldn't hurt," said my mom.

"You know, the *V*s have a very scrimpy section in the dictionary. It's full of good words, like *vicious* and *voracious*; but it could use some more."

Cinderella Smith

The More the Merrier

by

Stephanie Barden

Illustrations by

Diane Goode

HARPER

An Imprint of HarperCollinsPublishers

Library of Congress catalog card number: 2011933213
ISBN 978-0-06-200442-0 (pbk.)

Typography by Erin Fitzsimmons
13 14 15 16 17   LP/BR   10 9 8 7 6 5 4 3 2 1
❖
First paperback edition, 2013

1

A Turquoise Converse Sneaker

"It's time to leave for school!" I yelled to my mom and my little sister, Tess. And I knew this not because of the clock or because a show ended on TV. I knew it because I could hear the *bounce-bounce-bounce* of my next-door neighbor Charlie's basketball coming up our walkway.

"Hi, Tarlie!" Tess raced out the door first. She had a big, huge crush on Charlie and just couldn't wait to see him every morning.

"Hi, Tess!" said Charlie. "Hi, Tinder!"

I did a big sigh on account of the name he called me. When we were little, we couldn't say each other's names just right, so we called each other Tinder and Tarles. Now we can say the *s* and the *ch* sounds just fine, but Charlie keeps calling me Tinder to bug me.

Tess grabbed hold of my hand, and we followed Charlie, who was jogging and dribbling his basketball down the block. Every day we walk to school together, along with a kindergartner named Louie, who lives at the end of our block. Most times our moms come too because they're all friends. My mom brings Tess, and Louie's mom brings his little sister, Maggie. Charlie's mom just brings Charlie, though, because his big brother goes to another school on a bus.

"We're picking up Rosemary T.!" my mom called.

Charlie stopped where he was and waited for us to catch up.

Rosemary T. is another kid who lives on Blackberry Lane and goes to our school. She almost never walks, though. Her mom drives her big sisters to their school first, then drops Rosemary T. off at the end. Also, Rosemary T. does not like fresh air and exercise too much.

Since Rosemary T. didn't know that the dribbling

sound was the signal to come outside, Tess and I
went up to the front door and knocked.

"Is it raining?" Rosemary T. didn't look too happy.

"Nope," I said.

"I can't believe my mother is making me walk."

"My mom said she was sick," I said.

"Well then, I can't believe my *father* is making
me walk."

She said *father* very loud because right then he
was heading out the door with Rosemary T.'s sisters.

"I'm sorry, honey," said Mr. Taylor. "I don't have
time to get all of us where we need to be this
morning."

Rosemary T. made a big *harrumph* noise.

"Don't be such a baby," said her oldest sister.

Her middle sister rolled her eyes. "You only have
to walk a few blocks."

Rosemary T. rolled her eyes right back. "Whatever."

Mr. Taylor waved hello to everyone, and he and
Rosemary T.'s sisters all got in their car.

Louie and his mom and Maggie crossed the street
to join us, and we started off again to school.
Maggie grabbed my hand and Rosemary T.'s hand
and Louie grabbed Tess's hand, and we walked in a
big, long chain down the block.

"Skipping!" yelled Tess, so we started skipping.

"Singing!" yelled Maggie.

Right then the Taylors' car drove by and honked. Rosemary T. let go of Maggie's hand superquick, and our chain wobbled a little bit but then straightened out.

"Grab back on, Rosemary T.!" I yelled. "Don't get left in the dust!"

"Head, shoulders, knees, and toes," Louie sang.

"Head, shoulders, knees, and toes," Maggie and Tess and I joined in.

"Eyes and ears and mouth and nose," Charlie yelled, bouncing his ball all around us.

"Head, shoulders, knees, and toes," we sang all the way to school, except for Rosemary T.

When we got to the playground, she raced off to find her best friend, Rosemary W. I said good-bye to Tess and my mom and went to get in my class line because the start-of-school bell rang.

My best friend, Erin, was already in line behind the Rosemarys, so I went to stand by her.

"I had to *walk* to school today with *Cinderella*,"

Rosemary T. said to Rosemary W. The way she said it made it sound terrible.

"I'm right behind you, Rosemary T.," I said.

She turned around. "I can't believe you were *skipping* and *singing* and *holding hands* on the way to school."

"I can't believe you let go," I said.

"I would never want to look as babyish as you," she said.

"I would have skipped and sung and held hands," said Erin.

"I know you would," I said, "because the more the merrier!"

"I was so embarrassed," Rosemary T. told Rosemary W. "I walked way back with her mom and pretended I didn't know her."

"I would have done the same thing," said Rosemary W.

"You missed out," I said. "It was funderful!" I was very into making up new words lately, and this one was a combination of *fun* and *wonderful* all together.

"I hate all those dumb words you keep making up," said Rosemary T.

"It's very immature," said Rosemary W.

"It is not," said Erin.

"It is so," said Rosemary W.

"It's just another one of the childish things that Cinderella is always doing lately," said Rosemary T., "like hanging out with little kids and losing shoes."

My feelings started hurting like the dickens, and I felt tears filling up my eyes. Luckily our line started moving and the Rosemarys went ahead, so they didn't see.

"Didn't your moms ever teach you," Erin called after them, "that if you can't say something nice, you shouldn't say anything at all?"

I blink, blink, blinked at the tears walking to class and was good to go by the time we got there.

"Find your seats, class." Our teacher, Mr. Harrison, waited for us to get all settled. "As you know, our all-school spelling bee is a week from today. Now that you're in the third grade, the three best spellers among you will get to participate."

There were some hoorays from the good spellers and some groans from the not-so-good spellers. I myself didn't say anything because I'm somewhere in the middle.

"On Monday we'll have our in-class spelling bee to determine who those three are," said Mr. Harrison.

"To encourage you to study hard, whoever does the best in the all-school spelling bee will get to plan a class party."

Everyone hoorayed to that, because everyone loves a class party.

Zachary, a very, extremely quiet boy who sits at the back of the classroom, raised his hand.

"Yes, Zachary?" said Mr. Harrison.

I strained my ears to hear. Zachary doesn't say much, so when he does, I'm always very interested.

"What kind of a party?" he asked.

"What kind?" Mr. Harrison asked back.

"You know," said Zachary, "like a birthday party or a holiday party or a last-day-of-school party."

"It can be whatever kind of party the winner wants," said Mr. Harrison. "What are some things you're interested in? What would make a good party theme?"

"I don't know," said Zachary, very quiet again.

"I'm interested in dinosaurs," said Logan, "so I'd have a paleontology party."

Mr. Harrison wrote *Paleontology* on the blackboard.

"I'm interested in insects," said Trevor, "so I'd have some kind of bug theme."

"I'd do a Let Pluto Stay a Planet party," said

Christopher.

Mr. Harrison wrote *Bugs* and *Planet Pluto* on the board. "How about you, Cinderella?" he said.

I happened to share a table with Logan, Trevor, and Christopher, who happened to be the three smartest boys in the class. I guess Mr. Harrison wanted to finish up with our table, because I didn't have my hand up.

"I don't have the foggiest idea," I said.

Mr. Harrison looked like he could not believe his ears. "But you always have an idea."

"I know," I said. "Maybe it's more like I have too many foggy ideas and they're all running around inside my head and I can't decide on just one."

Mr. Harrison smiled and wrote *I Can't Decide Yet*. He added a check mark after it. "That check is for you, Zachary, since you can't decide yet either."

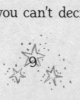

Zachary nodded.

Kristy raised her hand, and I knew for sure what her idea was going to be.

"Horses," she said.

I smiled across the room at Erin, and she smiled right back. Erin sat next to Kristy at a table with girls who were just crazy about horses. I could tell that Erin had known for sure what Kristy's idea was going to be like I did.

"Horses for me too," said Olivia, Kristy's best friend.

Mr. Harrison wrote *Horses* on the board and put a check mark next to it.

"I think it should be basketball," said Charlie.

"Or maybe soccer," said Jack. He sits next to Charlie at a table full of boys who are loud and love sports.

Kids started calling out party ideas, and Mr. Harrison wrote them all down.

"Ahem!" said Rosemary T. very loudly to get everyone's attention. "Our whole table agrees that it should be an I Believe in Unicorns party."

I looked over at her table. Rosemary W. and Hannah were nodding their heads. Abby, who also sat with them, didn't look so sure. Still she didn't

say anything out loud.

Mr. Harrison added *I Believe in Unicorns* to the long list of party ideas on the blackboard. He put three check marks next to it.

There was a knock on our classroom door, and the other third-grade teacher, Mrs. Kirk, poked her head in.

"Excuse me a moment, class." Mr. Harrison walked over to see what she needed.

"But I don't believe in unicorns," said Kristy. "They

aren't real horses."

Rosemary T. spun around in her chair and stared hard at Kristy. "Then you will definitely never be invited to join the I Believe in Unicorns Club."

Rosemary T. and Rosemary W. were very into starting clubs lately. To give you a few examples, there was the American Girls Club if you liked those books and the Sisters Club if you had at least one sister and the Grape Club if you thought that was the best flavor. There was also the Pierced Ears Club that I wasn't in because I don't have pierced ears yet. And the Dance Class Club that Erin wasn't in because she hasn't started dance class yet.

Rosemary T. kept up that mean stare at Kristy. "Also, when *I* win the spelling bee and *I* plan my I Believe in Unicorns party, you can just sit out in the hall."

"You won't get any unicorn cupcakes either," added Rosemary W.

Kristy blinked very fast at the tears in her eyes, but she started to cry anyway. Her whole table patted her on the back and told her it was okay, but that just made her cry harder. And right then and there I started to see red, which means I got mad with a capital *M*.

"Rosemary T.!" I stood up. "You owe Kristy an apology!"

The whole Rosemarys' table looked over at me very surprised.

"For one," I said, "you have to win the spelling bee before you can plan the party. For two, it's a class party, and everyone is included."

"Harrumph!" Rosemary T. said very loud.

"Harrumph!" Rosemary W. and Hannah said too.

"That must be the sound that a herd of magical unicorns makes," said Charlie.

Everyone started laughing, especially Kristy.

Mr. Harrison finished up talking to Mrs. Kirk and shut the door. "Cinderella, are you leaving us?"

I forgot I was standing up. "No, I'm staying." I sat back down.

"She couldn't go anywhere anyway," said Rosemary T. "She's not wearing one of her shoes."

I looked down, and only one of my turquoise Converse sneakers was on my feet. I wasn't too surprised, though. I have a habit of taking off my shoes when I'm sitting at my desk. This is A-OK with Mr. Harrison too as long as I put them on again before I go anywhere.

I was about to slip my shoe back on, but Rosemary T. was whispering to Rosemary W. and pointing at my feet. Instead, I pointed my toes like we do in dance class and waved right back at them with my sock feet underneath the table.

2

Vexylent

"Did you bring tuna fish again?" Rosemary T. asked when we got to the lunchroom.

"Yep." I put an empty seat between us so she wouldn't have to be too close to my sandwich. "It's my new favorite."

"It smells so gross," she said.

"You told me that yesterday," I said. "Just breathe through your mouth and you won't have to smell it."

"I have peanut butter and jelly." Rosemary W. sat in the empty seat between us.

"I have yogurt." Hannah sat across from Rosemary
T.

"Me too," said Rosemary T.

"I'll bring yogurt tomorrow," said Rosemary W.

Erin and Abby plunked their lunch trays down
across from me. I never bought lunch, so I was
always very interested to see what they were
serving. Today it was grilled cheese sandwiches and
carrots and orange slices.

"Hey, school lunch is all orange today," I said.

"Yeah," said Abby, "and it's all good too, no green
beans."

"Or peas," said Erin. "Cinderella, I'll trade you

half of my sandwich for half of yours."

"Deal." I handed her the half I hadn't bitten into.

"Now you'll be just as smelly as Cinderella," said Rosemary T.

"Cinderella isn't smelly," said Erin.

"After she eats tuna fish she is," said Rosemary W.

Erin looked at me and rolled her eyes and held up her tuna half.

I held up mine too, and we touched them together, just like when people toast with glasses.

"Cheers!" we said, and took a bite.

"*What* are you *doing*?" asked Hannah.

"We're cheers-ing," I said. "We always do that when we're eating the same stuff."

"It's just another stupid, childish, Cinderella thing," said Rosemary T.

My eyes started watering up again, and I blink, blink, blink, blinked. "You are so not-nice lately, Rosemary T."

Nobody said anything to that, and our part of the table got very quiet. Everyone kept eating, except me. I couldn't swallow on account of the lump of sad in my throat.

Rosemary T. finished her lunch and stood up. "Let's go."

Rosemary W. and Hannah stood up too and followed Rosemary T. over to the garbage can. Abby took one last bite, shrugged her shoulders, and followed them out of the lunchroom.

"I am getting very, extremely tired of Rosemary T. and all her meanness lately," I said.

"Lately?" said Erin. "She's been this way ever since I've known her." Erin was the new kid this year, so she had only known Rosemary T. for a little while.

"I guess she has been pretty mean all year, but she didn't used to be."

"She didn't?" asked Erin.

"Nope," I said. "We've lived by each other ever since we were born, and we were always pretty good friends."

"Wow," said Erin.

"But right about now I am very sad and mad at her," I said. "I would also really like to call her some bad names, if I was allowed."

"You mean like *dumb* and *rude* and *awful* and *stupid*?" asked Erin.

I nodded.

"I'm not allowed to say things like that either," she said.

"I guess *our* mothers *did* teach us that thing you said before."

"If you can't say anything nice, don't say anything at all?"

"Yep," I said. "And I can't think of one nice thing I'd like to say to Rosemary T. right now."

"Me neither," said Erin. "We might just have to stop talking to her."

I thought about that for a minute. "I think you're right. I think we're going to have to give her the silent treatment."

"Deal," said Erin.

"Deal," I said right back.

We headed out to recess and did not go play four-square with the Rosemarys. Instead we went and sat on our favorite bench by the basketball courts.

"Do you want to come over and study spelling this weekend?" asked Erin. "My stepdad got me a big book all full of spelling words."

"That would be awesome," I said.

"Wouldn't it be great if we both won and got to plan the class party together?"

"It would be so, so great!" I agreed.

"Even if we don't win," said Erin, "we have to beat the Rosemarys."

"Deal," I said. "Rosemary T. is a very good speller, though."

"We'll have to be careful she doesn't find out how hard we're studying," said Erin.

"It'll be our super top secret," I said.

"Yeah," said Erin. "I'll have my mom call your mom to make plans."

"Be sure to have your mom call tonight," I said. "My parents leave on their trip tomorrow."

"Your Aunt Flora is coming to stay, right?" said Erin.

"Right," I said. "It will be awesome."

"Flora's awesome." Erin knew that because my Aunt Flora was her dental hygienist.

"I'm glad you like her," I said. "Not everybody likes going to the dentist."

"Well, I do," said Erin. "I like the TV to watch while your teeth are getting clean and the prizes afterward."

"Me too." I had to yell, because the bell rang, saying lunch recess was over.

When we got into class, we had gym and then math and then Table Book Talks. That is something Mr. Harrison invented, and this is how it works. We read any book we want and then we take turns giving a book talk at our table, just like a real-life librarian. We're supposed to speak slowly and clearly so our audience can understand us and start with the title and author and the book's Main Theme. The Main Theme means what the book is mostly all about. Next we have to give a few examples that support the Main Theme. At the end of our talk we can recommend the book to our table if we think it was really good.

Logan went first.

"I'm reading *Dinosaur Dining* by Natalie Ann Westberg. It's mostly all about what dinosaurs used to eat, and that is the Main Theme. To give a few examples of this, *Diplodocus* was a herbivore, and *Megalosaurus* was a huge carnivore and might have been a scavenger too."

"Does *-ur-* before mean 'vegetarian'?" I knew *carnivore* meant "meat eater," but I wasn't sure about that *-ur-* thing.

"Yes," said Logan, "but it's *her-bivore*, you know, like herbs and plants."

"Got it," I said.

"I'm only to the *N*s," said Logan, "but I would highly recommend this book."

"It sounds vexylent." I tried out a new word I'd

just come up with then and there. Like I mentioned before, one of my favorite things to do nowadays is invent new words. When I come up with a really good one, I send it to the dictionary people and try to get them to add it.

Logan pricked up his ears because he likes vocabulary words too. "Is that good or bad?"

"Very, extremely excellent," I said.

He nodded.

Next went Trevor.

"I'm reading about *Ants from A to Z* by Malcolm Shure."

"Speak slower and clearer," said Christopher. "Jack is talking so loud I can't hear you."

Trevor started again. "I'm reading about *Ants from A to Z* by Malcolm Shure. It's mostly all about ants, but it does talk about bees a little; but ants are the Main Theme. It starts with army ants and ends with weaver ants. Those are my two examples."

"Does it talk about ant farm ants?" I asked. "Tess just got some, and we don't know much about them."

"I'm not sure," said Trevor. "I'll do some research and let you know."

"Thanks," I said.

"And also I would highly recommend this book," he added.

"It sounds vexylent," said Christopher.

I gave him a thumbs-up for using my word.

I was about to book talk my book, which was *Poppy and Rye* by Avi, but the bell rang and that meant it was the end of school.

"We'll finish up with these Monday," said Mr. Harrison. "Remember, next week is a busy one. There'll be spelling bees Monday and Friday, and in between we have visitors stopping in to tell us about their careers. Have a great weekend, everyone!"

Everyone told him to have a great weekend too, and we went out to get it started.

3

A Flying
Green Sneaker

"Can you take a picture of me and Tess jumping up and down and yelling?"

My mom's eyebrow went up, but only a little bit, which is just fine. It's the way she asks "Why?" without having to say it out loud.

"I want to include it in my letter to the dictionary people," I said.

My mom put a few more things in her suitcase and tried to close the lid. "What word are you suggesting this time?"

"*Vexylent*," I said. "I just came up with it yesterday during Table Book Talks. It's short for 'very, extremely excellent,' and I think having a picture of how it feels will help."

"I'm sure it wouldn't hurt," said my mom. "Can you sit on this so I can zip it up?"

I climbed up on her bed and then on top of her suitcase. "You know, the *V*s have a very scrimpy section in the dictionary. It's full of good words, like *vicious* and *voracious*; but it could use some more."

The zipper finally made it around just as Tess ran into the room.

"Woilà!" This time she remembered to put on her pants.

My mom held up the camera. "Say *cheese*."

"No! Act like something vexylent happened!" I said.

I climbed off the bed, and we started jumping up and down and yelling like our team just made a touchdown.

One of Tess's green sneakers flew off, and that got me wondering if Tess was going to have a problem with shoes like me. I vowed right then and there to keep an eye on her feet as much as I could. I also

vowed right then and there to name and address all her shoes like I always do to mine.

"Got it," said my mom. "Do you want me to print it up?"

"Yes, please!" I ran off to finish my letter superquick before Aunt Flora came.

The place that I ran off to was my bedroom, which looks very different nowadays. Last weekend we moved my old bed into Tess's room. It was time for her to have a bed without a bar across to keep her from falling out. I didn't mind one little bit either, because I got a brand-new bunk bed out of the deal. Now I have a place for a friend to sleep when I have sleepovers, which I just love to have, especially with Erin.

"Ta-da!" Tess ran into my room waving the printed-up picture of us feeling vexylent.

"Thank you." I sealed up the letter and followed her out to the living room.

My mom and dad were finishing getting ready, so Tess and I stood by our big front window and waited for Aunt Flora and her cat to arrive. I mean, WAITED FOR AUNT FLORA AND HER CAT TO ARRIVE! All in capitals! I have wanted a pet for my whole entire life, and now I got to have one for a whole entire week.

Aunt Flora's cat is named Miss Purvis. She's kind of an old-lady cat and is only a little bit friendly. When we go over to Aunt Flora's house, Miss Purvis will let us pet her for a few minutes, but then she gets up and leaves. If Tess follows after her and tries to pet her more, she hisses and swipes with her paw. I guess she might not be the greatest pet in the world; but she's still a pet, so who cares?

We are not allowed to have a pet for keeps at our house, and that is a great, big *Alas*. *Alas*, by the way, is something I say when I'm a little bit frustrated or a little bit sad. If you say it with a big, huge sigh, it makes you feel better; and that makes the *Alas* thing easier to take. Tess pointed over to Charlie's driveway, where he was practicing basketball in the pouring-down rain.

I shook my head and did a big sigh, because no normal person would be outside on a day like today. Tess shook her head and did a big sigh too.

My dad carried his suitcase into the living room. "Don't worry, Flora will be here soon."

I was about to tell him that we weren't sighing because of that when I heard the chugging, sputtery noise that the Flying Machine makes. That's what we call Aunt Flora's very old sports car since it

kind of sounds like a helicopter. It's bright orange and has round, froggy headlights that sort of roll open and shut. It used to go very fast, but now it's pretty slow; and it burps when you turn it off.

"I hear Flora." My mom set her suitcase down by my dad's.

As soon as the Flying Machine got quiet, we heard a big, loud, growly-meow coming all the way from my aunt's car. It kept going and going like it was never going to stop, and my mom's eyebrow went up and up like it was never going to stop either.

"Is that Miss Purvis?" asked my dad.

"I think so." My mom's eyebrow was still way up.

"Maybe you should give Flora a hand."

My dad ran out the front door to help, but Tess and I stayed back in the doorway. Part of me wanted to help too, but part of me didn't want to get all soaking wet. Charlie stopped practicing basketball and stared at my aunt's car. "Hi, Tinder! Hi, Tess!"

"Hi, Tarlie!" Tess yelled, and waved like mad.

My dad ran back toward the house carrying two suitcases, and my aunt followed carrying a cat carrier.

"Do you need any help?" called Charlie.

"No thanks, Charlie," my aunt called back. And FYI, she knew him because she cleans his teeth too, just like Erin's.

My aunt set down the cat carrier, and the millions of bracelets she wears jingled and jangled. She took off her black raincoat and was wearing all black underneath because that's her favorite color. Miss Purvis made a weird, yowly noise that sounded like Halloween.

My mom gave my aunt a big hug. "Thank you so much for watching the girls."

"And ants." Tess held out her new space-age ant farm all full of blue gel and ant tunnels.

My aunt kneeled down for a better look. "How cool is that!"

"It's vexylent," I said.

"It is," said my aunt. And that is one of the reasons I like her so much. She knew just what my new word meant without asking or anything.

"I like your bandanna," I said.

Aunt Flora looked a little bit like a pirate with her hair that's the same color as mine hiding under a scarf.

"Thank you," she said. "I like your shoes."

I was wearing one pink Skecher and one white Skecher because I couldn't find their mates.

Miss Purvis's Halloween yowls got louder, and my mom's eyebrow started to go up again.

"Is this too much to ask?"

"No way," said my aunt.

"We are all going to have a ball."

"Yep," I said, "because the more the merrier!"

My aunt smiled and tapped her nose, which is our fancy way of saying "You got it."

I tapped my nose back.

My mom's eyebrow was still up a little bit, but she and my dad gave us big hugs and kisses and headed out the door. Tess started to cry, and Aunt Flora picked Miss Purvis up out of her carrier and put her in Tess's arms. I think that cat was a little too heavy for Tess, though, because she sort of crumbled to the ground and Miss Purvis crumbled with her. Miss Purvis made the loudest Halloween yowl of all and raced out of the room. Then everything was quiet.

"Peace at last," said Aunt Flora.

"Is Miss Purvis okay?" I asked.

"She's fine," said my aunt. "She'll explore a little and then find a hiding place. Are you ready for lunch?"

"Yes!" Tess and I said at the same time.

"What are you in the mood for?" asked my aunt.

"How about breakfast?" I said. One of the very fun things about my aunt is that she likes to eat breakfast food any old time of the day and not just in the morning.

"Sure," she said. "How about we make Pancake Surprise?"

"What's that?" I asked.

"It starts off like regular pancakes," said Aunt Flora, "but then you add secret ingredients."

"Like what kind of secret ingredients?"

"Whatever you feel like," said my aunt. "That's what makes it a surprise."

"I like surprises," said Tess.

"Me too," I said.

"Well, let's get to work."

So we followed my aunt into the kitchen.

4

Purple Potion

I showed Aunt Flora where the pancake mix was way up high, and she reached it down. I measured out the water and only sloshed a little bit out on my way to the bowl.

"Do you want to stir?" I asked Tess.

"No, I have to go to the bathroom."

"Go for it," said Aunt Flora.

"I like company," said Tess.

"Okay," said my aunt. "Can you be in charge of the Pancake Surprise for a little while?"

"Sure!" I liked the idea of being in charge.

"Look through the fridge and the cupboards and add anything to the batter that you think would be good." Aunt Flora headed out of the kitchen.

I opened up the fridge and pulled out two bananas and a carton of blueberries. Next I scooped in some peanut butter and added a whole bunch of spices. Last I dribbled in ten drops of red food coloring to make the Surprise even more surprising.

"How's it coming, Cinderella?" my aunt called from the bathroom.

"Good," I said. "Except the Pancake Surprise is too thick to stir."

"Add some liquid and use your hands to mix it together," she said.

I put some milk into the bowl and started mashing the Pancake Surprise together with my hands. It turned a dark purple and so did I, all the way up to my elbows.

"Wow." Aunt Flora and Tess came back into the kitchen. "That's the most interesting Pancake Surprise I've ever seen."

"Should we eat it?" I stuck my nose down close and gave a big sniff. "It smells pretty good, even though it looks pretty weird."

"Sure we should." Aunt Flora put a pan on the stove and started heating some oil.

I went over to the sink and washed my hands. The batter came off, but the purple stayed on. I washed them again. "I think the Pancake Surprise turned me purple."

"I guess it was a Purple Potion instead," said Aunt Flora.

We sat down and ate the first batch of pancakes, which were actually pretty good.

"More!" said Tess.

"Okay." Aunt Flora went back to the stove and heated more oil.

A weird *knock-bounce-knock-bounce* noise came from the front door.

"What in the world is that?" asked Aunt Flora.

"That's Charlie. He can't do anything without his basketball." I did a big sigh and went to answer the door. Tess did a big sigh and followed me.

"Don't let Miss Purvis out!" called Aunt Flora.

I opened up the door a crack and kept it in place while we talked. "Hi, Charlie."

"Hi, Tarlie!" Tess yelled through the crack in the door.

"Why aren't you opening the door?" he asked.

"Because my aunt's cat isn't supposed to go outside," I said.

Miss Purvis came running and tried to push through the door with her nose. When it wouldn't budge, she started to yowl.

"That is one noisy cat," said Charlie.

Miss Purvis yowled louder and stuck her paw through the crack in the door.

"I should probably close the door," I said. "I don't want her to squeeze through."

"Okay," said Charlie. "My mom just told me to come over and tell Flora that if you need anything, we're right next door."

"I'll tell her." I reached my hand through the crack to scoop Miss Purvis's paw back in.

"Whoa!" said Charlie. "What happened to you?"

I'd forgotten I was purple. "I had a little problem in the kitchen."

"A *little* problem?" said Charlie.

"Purple Potion!" yelled Tess.

"No kidding," said Charlie.

I got Miss Purvis's paw through the crack and shut the door. "Bye, Charlie."

"See ya, Tinder and Tess!" Charlie's bounces faded down the front walk.

Tess skipped back to the kitchen. "Tinder and Tess! Tinder and Tess!"

"What did Charlie want?" asked my aunt.

"His mom sent him over to say, if you need anything, they're right next door."

"That was nice," said my aunt.

We sat down and ate more pancakes. We stuck out our tongues to see if they were turning purple, but only my hands and arms had changed.

The phone rang, and Aunt Flora answered it. "It's for you, Cinderella. It's Erin."

"Hi," said Erin. "Are you ready to come over and practice spelling?"

"Yep," I said. "We're just finishing up lunch."

While I waited to be picked up, I washed my hands over and over again and told Aunt Flora all about the spelling bee. Starting in first grade, every class has one, and the three best spellers get a ribbon. Once you're in third grade, the three best spellers get a ribbon and get to be in the all-school spelling bee. That one is very big and fancy. It's at night, so all the parents can come after work. The spellers get to be up on the stage in the lunchroom and get to talk into a microphone, which is something I myself have never done.

"Do your parents know about all this?" asked Aunt Flora.

"Yep," I said. "I'm supposed to call and tell them if I make it into the final, and they're going to try to change their flight and come home a day early. Do you think you can come?"

"Of course!" said Aunt Flora. "I was so sorry to have to miss your dance recital."

"You don't have to be sorry," I said. "You were

doing something very, extremely important."

And that was true. Aunt Flora had been helping fix people's teeth in some other country.

"Well, thank you for understanding," said Aunt Flora, "but I wouldn't miss your spelling bee for the world."

"If I make it, that is," I said.

"True," said Aunt Flora.

"There's something more too. Erin and I are planning on being the best spellers in our class. Whoever makes it the furthest in the all-school spelling bee gets to organize a party."

"That sounds like fun," said my aunt.

"Really, really fun," I said. "So you have to keep it super top secret that we're practicing, because we don't want anyone else to practice harder."

"My lips are sealed," said Aunt Flora.

Erin's mom honked her car horn out front, and I ran for the door.

"Don't let the cat out!" called Aunt Flora.

5

Mix-matched Skechers

When I jumped in the car, Erin said, "You're part purple! *P-u-r-p-l-e*."

"Yes, I am," I said. "*Alas. A-l-a-s*."

I told Erin and her mom all about the Pancake Surprise that turned into a Purple Potion.

Then I told them all about Miss Purvis.

"I can't wait to meet her," said Erin.

"I can't wait for you to meet her either," I said. "She's the kind of cat that's sort of picky, but I'm bound and determined to be her best friend by the end of the week."

Kitten!

We got to Erin's house and went right upstairs to her room to study. The big book full of spelling words was waiting for us on her bed, and she jumped up and pulled it onto her lap. I kicked off my one white Skecher and my one pink Skecher and jumped up next to her.

"I like your shoes," she said.

"I'm mix-matched today," I said.

"That reminds me," said Erin. "I found your sandal in my dress-up box."

"Hurray! That will make my mom very happy."

We opened up the spelling word book. There were four columns of words running down each page from the top to the bottom.

"It starts with first-grade words and goes all the way to fifth grade," said Erin.

K-i-t-t-e-n.

"Let's skip first and second," I said. "We should know those by now."

"Okay," said Erin. "We'll learn third for sure and then fourth and fifth if we can."

"Do you want to ask or spell first?" I asked.

"I'll ask," said Erin. "Your first word is *kitten*."

"That's a good one to start with," I said. "*Kitten. K-i-t-t-e-n. Kitten.*"

"Yes," said Erin. "Your next word is *fishing*."

Erin asked me twenty-seven words and I got them all right, except the bonus word, which was *invention*. Then it was my turn to ask.

"Your first word is *jeans*," I said.

"*Jeans*," said Erin. "*J-e-a-n-s. Jeans.*"

"That's right," I said. "But remember, there's also the other kind of genes, the ones inside us."

"Oh yeah," said Erin. "How do you know which kind they mean?"

"In the spelling bee you can ask for a definition or to have it put in a sentence," I said. "I learned that last year because I spelled *knew* wrong, but I got another chance."

"Okay," said Erin. "Please put *jeans* in a sentence."

"Certainly," I said. "Erin is wearing a new pair of jeans today."

"*Jeans*," said Erin. "*J-e-a-n-s. Jeans.*"

She got all the rest of her words right, even her bonus one, which was *amazed*.

We spent all afternoon going back and forth with the columns; but when it was time for me to go home, we had only made it through third grade. We wanted to keep studying, so I called Aunt Flora to see if Erin could spend the night.

"We'd love to have Erin over," said Aunt Flora. "The more the merrier!"

"Hey, that's what I say," I said.

"I know," she said. "I learned it from you."

When we got to my house, there were Chinese food cartons all over the dining-room table, and the house smelled de-licious with a capital *D*.

"Erin, Erin, Erin!" yelled Tess.

Erin picked her up and twirled her around.

Miss Purvis ran into the room to see what the commotion was.

"Hello." Erin bent down to pet Miss Purvis, but she just looked Erin up and down and stalked out of the room.

"I see what you mean about her being picky," said Erin.

"I'm so glad you could join us, Erin." Aunt Flora walked out of the kitchen with a handful of chopsticks.

"Awesome," I said. "I love those things, but I'm terrible with them."

"Me too," said Erin.

"Go wash your hands," said Aunt Flora. "Maybe some more of the purple will come off before we eat."

We raced to the bathroom, and I washed three times. "I think it's fading." I showed Erin.

"Maybe a little," she said.

We sat down, and Aunt Flora wrapped her fingers around her chopsticks and clacked them together. I tried to copy her, but the chopsticks felt wobbly in my fingers. She reached down to her plate, picked up a piece of chicken, and ate it. I reached down to my plate, picked up a piece of chicken, and spun it out of my chopsticks and onto the table.

Erin tried too, and chicken pieces kept plopping back down onto her plate. "When I was little, I did it this way." She put down one of her chopsticks and waved the other one around. "I pretended it was a magic wand and . . ." She stabbed the chopstick through a piece of chicken and held it up. "Ta-da!"

We all clapped.

"Me! Me!" yelled Tess, and she stabbed down on a piece of chicken too. "Ta-da!" She waved it over her head.

"It doesn't work with rice and noodles, though," said Erin.

"I'll go get us some forks." Aunt Flora headed into the kitchen just as the phone rang.

Tess ran and picked it up. "Hi!" she said, and then she nodded.

"You have to talk out loud," I said.

"Oh yeah," she said. "Yes. No." She hung up.

Erin and I burst out laughing as Aunt Flora came back into the room with a bunch of forks.

"Who was on the phone?"

"Rosemary T." Tess climbed back up into her chair.

"Who's that?" asked Aunt Flora.

"She's a girl in our class. She lives down the block," I said. "It's good you answered the phone, Tess, because I'm in the middle of giving her the silent treatment."

"Why?" My aunt gave us all forks and sat down.

"Because she's being very, extremely mean lately," I said.

"What has she done?"

"She says I'm childish and I embarrass her," I said. "And she won't let me be in her Pierced Ears Club."

"She won't let me be in her Dance Class Club either," said Erin, "even though I start next week."

"But we don't want to be mean right back to her," I said, "so we're giving her the silent treatment instead."

"Because if you can't say anything nice," said Erin, "you shouldn't say anything at all."

Aunt Flora was about to say something, but the phone rang.

"If that is Rosemary T. again," I said, "remember, I'm giving her the silent treatment because I don't want to be not-nice."

My aunt picked up the phone. "Hello? Oh hello, Rosemary T., Cinderella's busy at the moment. Can I take a message?"

Me and Erin looked at each other very surprised.

Grown-ups don't usually do things like that for kids.

"I'm sorry, but Cinderella has plans for tomorrow. She and Erin are practicing spell . . ."

Erin and me started shaking our heads like mad because Aunt Flora was about to tell the super secret. My aunt's eyes got all big, and she covered her mouth with her hand. She had just realized what she'd almost done. "Spells," she said. "They're practicing spells."

Tess turned the bag that the Chinese food had come in upside down, and fortune cookies spilled all over the table.

"And now it's fortune time," my aunt said, and she hung up. We all burst out laughing.

"Sorry, I almost blew it," said Aunt Flora.

Tess chose a fortune cookie, cracked it open, and handed the little white piece of paper to my aunt to read.

"'You will take a chance—and win,'" read Aunt Flora.

"Mine says: 'A pleasant surprise is waiting for you,'" said Erin.

"Mine is: 'You have common sense and a lot of charm,'" I said.

"That's a nice one," said my aunt.

"I'd rather get a surprise or win something," I said.

"Common sense and charm will get you far." My aunt got a serious look on her face. "You know, giving Rosemary T. the silent treatment might work for a while, but you'll have to talk to her eventually."

"Why?" I asked.

"Because it will start to get too awkward," she said. "Like the phone call tonight."

I thought about what she was saying and knew she was right. If my mom had been here when Rosemary T. called, she would have made me talk to her for sure. "But I don't have anything good to say."

"Don't you want to discuss what's going on with the two of you?" asked my aunt. "Don't you want to try to figure out what the problem is?"

"I'm not sure," I said.

"You have to do what feels right to you," said Aunt Flora. "But sometimes you get pushed too far, and you have to tell someone what's what."

"What's that mean?" I asked.

"It means telling someone how you're really

feeling," said my aunt, "clearing the air."

"I guess clear air would be good," I said. "But I'm hoping it will clear up all on its own."

"It might," said my aunt.

"I mean, Rosemary T. used to be nice, and she could be nice again. Then I wouldn't have to have a what's what at all."

"This is where your common sense is going to come in handy." Aunt Flora broke open her fortune cookie. "'All your hard work will pay off,'" she read.

"I wish I'd gotten that one," I said.

"Why?" she asked.

"Because maybe it would be about the spelling bee. Maybe all our studying would pay off in us winning."

"Well, in that case"—Aunt Flora handed me her fortune—"it's yours."

6

Great with a Capital G

We studied for a while and then watched Animal Planet with Tess. It was hard, though, because she asked a million zillion questions. Finally my aunt put her to bed.

"Peace at last," I said.

"It is awfully quiet," said Aunt Flora. "Miss Purvis must love her new hiding place."

The three of us settled in to watch *The Wizard of Oz*. That is one of my all-time favorite movies, but I don't get to watch it too much because the witch and the flying monkeys scare the dickens out of Tess.

When it was time for us to go to bed, we found out just where Miss Purvis's new hiding place was. It was right on my top bunk! She was at the end where my feet go, mixed in between a Lego pirate ship and a Playmobil castle. She opened one eye and stared at me, but she didn't get up to leave.

"It would be so great if she slept here all night." I climbed under the covers and made sure my feet didn't push into her.

Erin turned off the light and climbed into the bottom bunk. "I really like your new bed."

"Me too," I said.

"Do you usually sleep on the top or the bottom?"

"I go back and forth," I said. "If my toys are spread out too much up here, I sleep down there."

"Why do you keep some toys up there?" asked Erin.

"Because of Tess," I said. "Sometimes she knocks things over and breaks stuff apart."

Erin didn't talk for a minute. "Do you like having a little sister?"

"Most of the time," I said. "But sometimes she's a pest."

"I hope Anna and Julia don't think I'm a pest," said Erin.

Anna and Julia were Erin's new stepsisters that were away at college.

"Just don't wreck things they're working on or ask too many questions when they're watching TV."

"I won't," said Erin.

"I know," I said. "When are you going to see them again?"

"They're going to spend part of winter vacation with us."

"That will be fun," I said.

"Yeah." Erin got quiet again.

"Are you asleep?" I asked.

"No," she said. "I was just thinking. What kind of things do you like to do with Tess?"

"Hmm." I thought a little bit. "I like going places with her, like the library and the park. And I like teaching her stuff when she wants to learn."

"I'd like to go places with Anna and Julia and have

them teach me stuff," said Erin. "What else?"

I started to think about what else I liked to do with Tess, but on accident I fell asleep. I guess Erin did too, though, because she didn't ask me any more about it.

When I woke up the next morning, Miss Purvis was still right at the end of my bed. I crawled down to where she was and petted and petted her.

"You are a great cat," I whispered to her. "I think we're getting to be very good friends."

When Erin woke up, she asked if we could have Pancake Surprise for breakfast, and that was A-OK with everyone else. This time we made it much less surprising. We didn't add any food coloring or spices, just applesauce and raisins and some crumbled-up Nilla Wafers. The pancakes were a little crunchier than usual, but still pretty good.

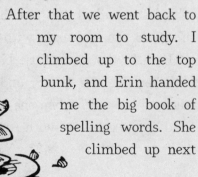

After that we went back to my room to study. I climbed up to the top bunk, and Erin handed me the big book of spelling words. She climbed up next and we got all settled, and Miss Purvis still didn't move at all.

"You ask first this time," said Erin.

"Okay," I said. "Fourth-grade words, here we come. Your first word is *January*."

"*January*," said Erin. "*J-a-n-u-a-r-y. January*."

"You spelled it right," I said, "but don't forget you have to add the capital."

"Oh yeah," said Erin. "*January*. Capital *J-a-n-u-a-r-y. January*."

"Hello," I said.

"Hello," Erin said back.

"No, *hello* is your next word."

"Oh!" Erin laughed. "*Hello. H-e-l-l-o. Hello*."

Erin got the rest of the words right in her column and then it was time for her bonus word. "*Entertain*," I said. "Let me entertain you by asking you how to spell things."

"Ooh," said Erin. "*Entertain. E-n-t-e-r-t-a-n-e* or *a-i-n*?"

"*A-i-n*." I handed her the book.

"Your first word is *flavor*," said Erin. "The best flavor is orange. I lied to get into the Grape Club."

"Hah!" I said. "Flavor. *F-l-a-v* . . . Is it *e-r* or *o-r*?"

"*O-r*," said Erin.

"*O-r*," I said. "I like cherry better than grape, by the way."

"Hah!" Erin said. "Your next word is two words. *United States.*"

"*United States,*" I said. "*U-n* . . . Wait, let me start over. Capital *U-n-i-t-e-d* capital *S-t-a-t-e-s. United States.*"

"That's right," said Erin.

I did pretty well on my column and only missed a couple, including my bonus word, which was *Antarctica,* because I forgot a *c* in the middle.

Erin handed me the book.

"Your first word this time is *panda,*" I said.

"I love panda bears," said Erin. "*P-a-n-d-a.*"

"Me too," I said.

"Hey," said Erin. "Panda bears might be a good theme for the class party."

"Yeah, "I said, "or maybe polar bears or sun bears or just plain bears."

"Or maybe the theme could be all zoo animals," said Erin.

"Or just all animals," I said.

"I guess there are a lot of great party ideas," said Erin. "I know why you couldn't decide at school."

There was a knock at my bedroom door.

"Come in," I said.

My aunt poked her head in. "Sorry to disturb you girls, but I'd like to start some laundry. Can you keep an eye on Tess for a few minutes? She's coloring with markers at the coffee table, and I don't want her to get carried away."

"Sure," I said.

"Thank you." Aunt Flora carried a big laundry basket down to the basement, and we went out to the living room.

"Hello!" said Tess.

"*H-e-l-l-o. Hello,*" I said.

"What's that?" Erin pointed to Tess's ant farm, which was sitting on the coffee table.

"My ants' house. They're watching me color while Aunt Flora does laundry."

We sat down by Tess and watched her color too until someone rang the doorbell. Miss Purvis streaked past us, and we all followed her to the front door. I opened it just a crack and peeked through. It was Rosemary T.! Without thinking, I shut the door back up.

"Hey!" Rosemary T. yelled from the other side of the door.

Erin and I looked at each other like we didn't know what to do.

"We probably can't give her the silent treatment right now," Erin whispered.

"Maybe she's all back to normal," I whispered back.

Rosemary T. knocked again, this time harder and louder. My heart was knocking too. "Someone open this door right now!" There was a thud that sounded like maybe Rosemary T. had kicked the door with her foot.

"Maybe not," I whispered.

"I'll take a break from the silent treatment." Erin opened up the door a crack. "Hello."

"Finally!" said Rosemary T. "I think Cinderella's dumb little sister slammed the door in my face, just like she hung up on me last night."

"Did not!" yelled Tess.

"Did so!" yelled Rosemary T. "Open the door!"

"I can't," said Erin.

"Well, go get Cinderella then," said Rosemary T.

"She's busy at the moment," said Erin.

Miss Purvis started yowling.

"What is that?" demanded Rosemary T.

"Flora's cat," said Erin.

"It sounds mean," said Rosemary T.

"She's pretty nice," said Erin.

"Whatever," said Rosemary T. "My mom made me come down here to return a book."

Miss Purvis stuck her paw through the crack in the door and yowled louder.

Rosemary T.'s voice moved away. "It's trying to scratch me!"

"No she's not," said Erin.

"Yes, it is!" yelled Rosemary T. "Close the door so it can't get out."

I picked Miss Purvis up and pulled her paw inside. Erin shut the door.

"Don't open the door until I'm gone," yelled Rosemary T. "I'll leave the book on the mat."

Aunt Flora came up from the basement. "What's going on?"

"Rosemary T. was just here," I said, "and we had to answer the door."

"Of course," said my aunt.

"And since we couldn't both give her the silent treatment," said Erin, "I talked."

"And then Miss Purvis scared her away." I rubbed

my chin on top of Miss Purvis's head, and she started to purr.

"Oh dear," said Aunt Flora. "Miss Purvis, you are a bad cat."

"No, she's not," I said. "She's a great, great, great, great cat, with a great big capital *G*."

7

Orange Crocs

I was very, extremely nervous to go to school on Monday for two reasons. One, it was the day for the classroom spelling bee; and two, I would have to see Rosemary T. I wanted to keep ignoring her and giving her the silent treatment, so I hoped she wouldn't push me too far. I really did not want to have a what's what if I could help it.

When I got to the playground, Erin ran over right away. "Are you all *r-e-a-d-y*. *Ready?*"

"I think so," I said, "but I'm not for sure."

Our class lined up to head into the school, and Charlie bounced his basketball right up behind us. "Rosemary T. told everyone playing basketball that your mom and dad are gone and there's crazy, weird stuff going on at your house."

We all three laughed the whole way into class.

"Good Monday morning," said Mr. Harrison. "Before we start our classroom spelling bee, we have a little business to attend to. Our special visitor tomorrow is Rosemary T.'s dad, and on Wednesday it's Jack's grandfather. Unfortunately, our special visitor for Thursday had to cancel. If any of you knows someone who might like to come and fill in, let me know."

I raised my hand but kept it hidden up inside my sleeve. A lot of the purple was gone, but not all of it. "My aunt might. She's a dental hygienist, and she's taking care of us while my mom and dad are gone."

"Not her aunt!" Rosemary T. whispered very loud so I could hear.

I looked over at her table, and now she was whispering quietly to Rosemary W. and Hannah and Abby. They started giggling.

"Having your aunt visit would be excellent," said Mr. Harrison. "Let's talk more about it after recess. Now, everyone, please get out a piece of paper and a pencil."

The spelling bee started with everyone taking a regular old spelling test at their desks. We did a self-correct when it was over and had to be very honest. If we missed less than five, we got to be in the front-of-the-class spelling bee.

The smart boys' table got to all be up front, including me. So did Erin and Kristy and Olivia. Charlie and Jack from the loud sports boys' table were up front and so was the whole Rosemarys' table. There were two arty girls and two stamp-collecting girls and last but not least was quiet Zachary.

We just lined up however we wanted to, and Erin and Abby made a space for me in between them.

"Cinderella's not wearing her shoes," Rosemary T. tattled.

I ignored Rosemary T. and didn't look at her at all, but I did race back to my table and put my orange Crocs back on.

The spelling bee started, and two people got out before I even got my first word.

"Okay, Cinderella," said Mr. Harrison. "Your first word is *coach*."

"*Coach*," I said. "*C-o-a-c-h. Coach*."

"Good," said Mr. Harrison. "Erin, your first word is *dream*."

"*Dream*," said Erin. "*D-r-e-a-m. Dream*."

"Good," said Mr. Harrison.

Erin and I smiled at each other.

Four more people got out before my next turn.

"Cinderella, your word is *camera*."

"*Camera*," I said. "*C-a-m-e-r-a. Camera*."

Erin got her next word right, which was *thumb*; but Abby and Hannah and three other people got out before it was my turn again.

My next word was *February*, and I got it right and remembered to add the capital and the weird *r*. Erin's next word was *foreign*, and she missed it. *Alas*. She walked to her seat and looked at me all sad, and I looked back at her just the same.

"Rosemary W.," said Mr. Harrison, "your word is *spoil*."

"*S-p-i-o-l*," spelled Rosemary W.

"That is incorrect," said Mr. Harrison. "Please sit down."

I was very happy about that, even if that wasn't very nice. If my best friend was out, at least Rosemary T.'s best friend was out too.

When it was my turn again, there were five of us left: Logan, Rosemary T., Charlie, Zachary, and me. That meant maybe we'd be having a paleontology party or an I Believe in Unicorns party or a basketball party or an I Can't Decide Yet party since me and Zachary still couldn't decide. I guess any of them would be okay, but I really wanted to win. I wanted Erin and me to get to pick a fun theme and plan everything out. And I wanted to beat Rosemary T.

"Cinderella?" said Mr. Harrison.

"Sorry," I said. "I was a million miles away."

"Sometimes that happens," said Mr. Harrison. "Your word is *witch*."

"Could you use it in a sentence, please?" I asked.

"The witch cast a spell on the teacher so she could win the spelling bee." Mr. Harrison bounced on his toes and smiled big.

"Abracadabra." I waved my hands at him.

Everyone laughed, especially Mr. Harrison.

"This is serious!" Rosemary T. stamped her foot. "You shouldn't make jokes during a spelling bee."

"So sorry," said Mr. Harrison. "Do you want me to repeat the word, Cinderella?"

"Nope, that's okay. *Witch. W-i-t-c-h. Witch.*"

Charlie got out next by forgetting one of the *t*'s in *attitude*, and Logan got out by giving *ceiling* an *ie* instead of an *ei*. That left Rosemary T., Zachary, and me, all on our way to the big spelling bee on Friday. And that was vexylent and awshucksible at the same time. And *awshucksible* is another word I invented that means "aw, shucks, that's terrible," FYI.

At the end of school, Kristy and Olivia ran up to me and Erin on the playground. "It's all up to you, Cinderella," they said.

"What is?" I asked.

"The spelling bee," said Kristy.

"You have to beat Rosemary T. and Zachary," said Olivia.

"We don't want to have an I Believe in Unicorns party," said Kristy. "And we bet your I Can't Decide Yet party will be way more vexylent than Zachary's."

I gave her a thumbs-up for saying my word, and she gave me a thumbs-up back.

"I wish I didn't get out." Erin had been saying that all day.

"Me too." I'd been saying that all day too.

We lined up against the fence with all the other kids that were getting picked up by car. The Rosemarys were lined up near us and were busy whispering and pointing. Me and Erin were busy ignoring them with a capital *I*.

"Good job on the spelling bee today, girls." Mr. Harrison stopped in front of us on the way to his car. "Cinderella and Rosemary T., I hope you'll make our class proud on Friday."

"We will," I said.

"I will," Rosemary T. said at the same time. "Do you believe in unicorns, Mr. Harrison?"

A loud, sputtering sound came from around the

corner, and Aunt Flora's car appeared. "Would you look at that!" said Mr. Harrison.

"That's my aunt's car," I said.

"I haven't seen an Opel GT in years."

"It sounds like a helicopter," I said, "so we call it the Flying Machine."

The Rosemarys started giggling, but it didn't sound nice.

Aunt Flora pulled up, and Mr. Harrison opened up the passenger door.

She looked at him very surprised. "Can I help you?"

"Hi, Aunt Flora." I climbed into the backseat. "This is my teacher, Mr. Harrison."

"Hello," said Mr. Harrison. "We're inviting visitors into our classroom this week, and a little bird told me you might be able to come in Thursday and talk about the dental world."

"I'd love to," said Aunt Flora.

"Great!" Mr. Harrison looked all around inside the car. "I didn't think Opel GTs had backseats."

"They didn't come with them," said Aunt Flora. "But the person I bought it from had kids, so she had one installed."

"Lucky for me and Tess," I said.

"Could you make the headlights pop up?" asked Mr. Harrison.

My aunt pulled hard on a lever, and the headlights rolled open.

Mr. Harrison whistled, and a car honked behind us.

"Sorry!" He shut the door and waved, and we drove off.

8

A Long Story

"I talked to my mom and dad last night, and they changed their flight so they can be home for the spelling bee," I told Erin. "They might be a little late, though, so I can't get out too early." We were hiding under her umbrella, waiting for the start-of-school bell. If it had been raining just a little bit harder, they would have opened the doors early and let us in. This was just a little bit of rain, though, that we call dribbly-spit, so we were stuck outside.

"Did you study last night?" Erin had loaned me

her big book of spelling words so I could keep practicing.

"Yep," I said. "I had my aunt quiz me for almost a half hour, and I started reading my mom and dad's big, huge dictionary too. I'm up to *academic*."

"Great," said Erin. "You have just got to win that spelling bee!"

The bell finally rang, and we were first in line.

Charlie got in line behind us. "I forgot to ask you yesterday; how's the purple?"

I pushed the sleeves of my raincoat and sweatshirt up. "I'm almost back to normal."

"You could never be normal." Jack got in line behind Charlie.

"She means a normal color," said Charlie. "You should have seen her on Saturday after the Purple Potion disaster."

"What potion disaster?" Rosemary T. and Rosemary W. got in line behind Charlie and Jack and of course butted into our conversation.

I pulled my sleeves down and faced forward.

"The potion disaster she had with her aunt," said Charlie. "Tell her, Cinderella."

"I happen to be ignoring Rosemary T. and giving her the silent treatment at the moment," I said.

"Why?" asked Rosemary T.

I kept facing forward.

"Why are you?" asked Charlie.

"It's a long story," I said, "so I don't even know where to begin."

"Tell me!" demanded Rosemary T.

"She can't tell you," said Jack, "because she's giving you the silent treatment."

I gave him a thumbs-up.

"Does this have something to do with your aunt?" asked Rosemary T.

"What does Flora have to do with anything?" asked Charlie.

"All this weird stuff started when her aunt came," said Rosemary T.

"It started way before that," said Erin.

I gave Erin a thumbs-up. It was a vexylent thing that she wasn't giving Rosemary T. the silent treatment 100 percent of the time, because sometimes it was almost impossible to do.

"The Rosemarys are getting on my nerves," said Erin.

We looked over to where they

were eating at the other third-grade lunch table. Even though we were sitting as far away from them as we could, we could still see they were whispering and staring at us.

"I guess it's getting a little awkward," I said. "Maybe giving Rosemary T. the silent treatment isn't helping her get back to normal."

Erin dipped a Tater Tot in ketchup and handed it to me. I made a cheese cracker sandwich and handed it to her.

"Thank you," we both said at the same time.

"Does anyone want to trade a pretzel for something?" asked Kristy.

"How about an apple slice?" said Olivia.

"How about a cheese and cracker?" I said.

She handed us both a pretzel, and we handed her back an apple slice and a cracker sandwich.

"To ignore someone and give them the silent treatment is one of the worst things ever!" Rosemary

T. said very loudly. "It's babyish and childish."

I looked over and saw she had a crowd of girls all around her. Hannah and Abby got up from the table and walked over.

"Rosemary T. sent us over to ask you why you're giving her the silent treatment."

I sat there and felt very, extremely awkward and embarrassed and didn't say anything.

"Are you giving us the silent treatment too?" asked Abby.

"Oh no," I said.

"Good," said Abby. "So what's going on?"

"It's a long story," I said.

Abby sat down, but Hannah ran back over to the Rosemarys. Kristy and Olivia and their friend Casey, who also loves horses, scooted closer.

I swallowed. "I don't even know where to begin."

Hannah marched back over. "Rosemary T. demands to know the whole long story."

"Once upon a time," said Erin.

Hannah made a big *harrumph* noise and ran back to the Rosemarys.

"There's that unicorn again," said Kristy.

We all started laughing.

"Well, I don't have time to deal with this babyish nonsense right now. Please tell Cinderella that I'm giving her the silent treatment too!" Rosemary T. stood up. "My daddy, the special visitor, is on his way." She marched out of the lunchroom, and Rosemary W. and some other girls followed. Hannah walked back over to our table.

"Rosemary T. said to tell you . . . ," said Hannah.

"I heard her," I said.

"She might not be talking to you," Erin said, "but she talks so loud it doesn't matter."

Hannah's mouth popped open, and she raced out of the lunchroom.

Abby stood up and looked like she didn't know what to do for a minute. Then she finally followed after Hannah.

9

A Clog with Puppy Teeth Marks

At school on Wednesday, while we waited for Jack's grandpa to get there, we wrote thank-you cards to Rosemary T.'s dad for coming to visit us.

"Try to win the spelling bee, Cinderella," said Logan.

"Yeah," said Trevor. "Whatever your party is, it will be way more vexylent than a unicorn party."

I gave him a thumbs-up for using my word.

"If Rosemary T. wins, she'll probably make us

swear allegiance to all unicorns before we can start the party," said Christopher. "If we refuse, she'll probably send us into the hall."

"And then some people would start to cry again," said Trevor.

"That would be awshucksible," I said.

"What's that?" asked Logan.

"Aw, shucks, that's terrible."

Logan nodded, and we started back working on our cards.

"If Zachary wins," said Trevor, "his party would probably be okay."

"Except he might forget to plan it," said Logan, "like he always forgets his homework and his lunch."

"Tess forgot her pants the other day," I said.

The smart boys started laughing very hard.

"Mr. Harrison," called Rosemary T. "We are working on something very important right now, and I think everyone should be serious."

"Oh, I think a little levity is always a good thing," said Mr. Harrison.

"What's *levity* mean?" asked Logan.

"It means 'humor, lightheartedness,'" said Mr. Harrison.

"Really, really try to win the spelling bee,

Cinderella," Logan whispered. "If Rosemary T. wins, she'll probably make a rule that there can't be any levity at her party."

"Five more minutes, class," said Mr. Harrison.

"I think hearing about firefighting from Jack's grandpa will be way more vexylent than hearing about banks," said Christopher.

I smiled big. My word was starting to get used a lot, and I was very, extremely happy about that.

"Yeah," said Logan. "But I did like the penny roll thing Rosemary T.'s dad gave us."

That reminded me. I wanted to ask Aunt Flora if she could bring in some kind of party favor thing to class too. Those penny rolls had been a big hit.

And then Jack's grandpa got there, and it was time to give him a warm welcome. He clomped into the classroom wearing big boots and a helmet, and right behind him was his dog!

I could not stop myself from staring at that dog. For one thing, I love dogs. But for two things, he was all black, not white with black spots. I started to worry that he'd gotten his fur burned in a fire; and even though it wasn't time for questions, I almost had to raise my hand and interrupt.

Luckily, quiet Zachary interrupted instead. "He doesn't look like a firefighting dog."

"You're right," said Jack's grandpa. "His name is Ashes, and he's a black Lab."

"Phew," I said out loud on accident.

Jack's grandpa laughed. "Firefighters have all kinds of dogs now, not just Dalmatians."

"How come?" asked Charlie.

"When firefighters used to get to fires in horse-drawn wagons, Dalmatians were good at keeping the horses calm," said Jack's grandpa. "But we don't use horses anymore, and we don't bring dogs to fires. Now we can have whatever kind of dog we want."

Ashes had been sitting quietly by Jack's grandpa's feet, but he started whining and pulling on his leash.

"Ashes likes to explore new places," said Jack's grandpa. "Is it okay with everyone if I let him wander around?"

"I'm allergic to dogs," said Rosemary T.

"You're not allergic to our dog," said Abby.

"Only big ones," said Rosemary T.

"Why don't you sit at my desk," said Mr. Harrison. "I'll make sure Ashes doesn't get too close to you."

Rosemary T. circled wide around Ashes and sat in Mr. Harrison's chair. As soon as she was settled, Jack's grandpa let go of Ashes's leash, and he started roaming around the classroom. He walked around tables and sniffed at people's backpacks and let them pet him when he walked by. I tried to pay attention to everything Jack's grandpa was saying, but Ashes kept distracting me. He took a long time getting to our table; but when he finally did, he got very interested in my clogs. He sniffed and sniffed and licked the one that was covered in puppy teeth marks from when Ralph, our neighbor's dog, had stolen it. Finally he plopped down right next to me and stuck his nose into my clog as far as it would go and let out a big sigh.

The whole classroom laughed, and I looked up. I had been so busy watching Ashes that I didn't realize that everyone else was watching him too.

"It looks like he found a good spot," said Jack's grandpa.

I reached down and gave Ashes some rubs.

"It looks like he's in love with Cinderella's smelly shoe," said Jack.

"Or maybe he's just in love with Cinderella," said Jack's grandpa.

The class made a big *Ooooh* noise, and I decided to set the record straight.

"He's not in love with me. I bet he just likes the warm heater, and he thinks my clog is a dog toy. My aunt's cat has been staying with us this week, and she likes warm places and toys too."

"So does my hamster," said Zachary, so I guess his quietness is maybe going away.

"So does our dog, Fletcher," said Abby.

I looked over at her and smiled.

"My snake likes warm places," said Trevor, "but he doesn't like toys."

Half the class said "Awesome" about Trevor's snake and the other half said "Ooh, yuck."

"Order! Order!" called Mr. Harrison.

84

Which we did, but then it was time for Jack's grandpa to go. And it was very sad, because Ashes had to leave and he did not want to one bit. Jack's grandpa had to sort of drag him out by his leash, and he almost made it out of the classroom with my clog in his mouth. Luckily Charlie noticed and got it back.

"Parting is such sweet sorrow," said Mr. Harrison. "But we'll have another exciting visitor tomorrow, right, Cinderella?"

"Right," I said.

"Will your aunt pick you up today in her Flying Machine?" he asked.

"Yep," I said. "She's picking up me *and* Rosemary T."

I heard a big gasp from the Rosemarys' table, so I guess Rosemary T. didn't know Aunt Flora was driving to dance class today.

"I'd be gasping too, Rosemary T., if I got to go for a ride in that car." I guess Mr. Harrison couldn't tell that was a bad gasp and not a good one.

I myself did not care one little bit that Rosemary T. didn't want to carpool with me. I didn't want to carpool with her either. I figured since Erin was starting dance class, she and I would carpool together instead. But because Rosemary T. and I lived right down the block from each other, the carpool had to stay the way it was. And that was way bigger than an *Alas!* or an Awshucksible. That was a YUCK-ICK-BLECH! All in capitals.

10

Phew!

Mr. Harrison was so crazy about that car that he walked me and Rosemary T. all the way to the fence to wait for Aunt Flora. He was all full of questions too. To give you a few examples, he asked if it used regular or unleaded gas and how many miles it got to the gallon. The bad news was, I didn't know any of the answers. The good news was, he talked so much that it wasn't awkward at all that Rosemary T. and I were giving each other the silent treatment. *Phew!* When we heard the Flying Machine's sputtering sound, Mr. Harrison started bouncing on his toes. He practically ran to open the door when Aunt Flora pulled up. I climbed right in and buckled up, but Rosemary T. did not move from the fence.

"Let's go, Rosemary T.; you don't want to keep this car waiting," said Mr. Harrison.

Rosemary T. looked down the fence to Rosemary W., who was still waiting to be picked up. They both rolled their eyes at each other, and Rosemary T. slouched into the car.

"Hi, Rosemary T.," said my aunt. "I'm Flora."

"Oh," said Rosemary T.

I saw my aunt's eyebrows go up a little bit in the rearview mirror. "How was school?"

Rosemary T. didn't say anything, so I did. "It was great. Jack's grandpa was our special visitor. He's a fireman, and he came wearing all his gear and he brought his dog."

"Was it a Dalmatian?" asked Aunt Flora.

"No," I said. "I thought it would be too, but it was a black Lab named Ashes. He was so cute like you wouldn't believe."

"Harrumph." Rosemary T. made her unicorn noise.

"Are you more of a cat person, Rosemary T.?" asked Aunt Flora.

"No." Rosemary T. was staring hard at the five earrings in my aunt's ear and the little diamond in her nose.

I thought about mentioning that Aunt Flora could be in the Pierced Ears Club, but then I remembered I wasn't talking to Rosemary T. Also, we pulled up in front of dance class just then.

"Thank you, Aunt Flora," I said.

"You're welcome," she said. "I'll be picking you up too."

"Why?" Rosemary T. looked a little sick to her stomach.

"Something came up for your mom." Flora gave a little wave, and her bracelets jangled.

We walked over to Miss Akiyama, who always waits in front for everyone to arrive.

"Hello, girls," she said. "You can go on in and get ready."

Rosemary T. raced inside.

"I think I'll just wait for my best friend, Erin, to get here," I said. "She's brand-new, and I want to introduce you."

Erin's car pulled up, and Erin and Emma and Nicole piled out. Emma and Nicole are in the other third-grade class, by the way. They live close to

Erin, so they got to carpool together, lucky pucks.

I introduced Miss Akiyama to Erin and then brought her inside and showed her all around. I'd been teaching Erin all sorts of warm-up positions and tap dance steps, and I think Miss Akiyama was very impressed. She told Erin "Good job" when class was over, and Miss Akiyama is always serious and doesn't usually talk like that.

"How was dance class?" Aunt Flora asked when we climbed back in the Flying Machine to drive home.

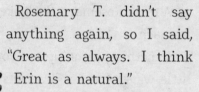

Rosemary T. didn't say anything again, so I said, "Great as always. I think Erin is a natural."

I thought Rosemary T. might *harrumph* again, but instead she said, "This car smells funny."

I took a big, long sniff, but I didn't smell anything.

"Does it smell like gas?" asked Aunt Flora. "I just filled it up."

"Speaking of gas," I said, "Mr. Harrison wanted to know what kind you use."

"I use regular," said Aunt Flora.

"It doesn't smell like gas," said Rosemary T.

"Does it smell dentist office-y?" I forgot I wasn't talking to Rosemary T. for a minute.

"No," said Rosemary T. "It's giving me a headache."

"Good thing we're home." Aunt Flora pulled up in front of Rosemary T.'s house.

Charlie was walking by carrying the Hansens' dog, Ralph. He smiled at us, and Ralph started wriggling. I asked if I could get out too and walk the rest of the way home with them.

"Sure," said Aunt Flora.

"Hey, you missed the chase," said Charlie.

"Sorry." I scooped up Ralph so Charlie's arms could have a break.

"Thanks." Charlie started shaking out his arms. "He's getting heavier."

The Ralph that was getting heavier was the same Ralph that stole my clog and left his puppy teeth marks in it, by the way. He's a brownish, fluffy dog who's a very good escape artist and a very fast runner. And that is an awshucksible combination.

"I can't believe you got to ride in Flora's car," Charlie said to Rosemary T.

"Got to?" said Rosemary T. "You mean *had* to. Twice."

I started walking to the Hansens with Ralph in

my arms so I wouldn't have to listen to Rosemary T. anymore.

"Had to?" I heard Charlie say. "You are so weird."

He ran and caught up with me.

Rosemary ran to catch up too. "I am not weird," she said all offended.

"Yes, you are," said Charlie.

"If anyone's weird, it's Cinderella's family."

"We're not weird!" I said.

"Yes, you are!" said Rosemary T. "You hang up on people and slam doors in people's faces. Where are your manners?"

"Most of the time we have good manners," I said.

"You also refuse to talk to people and that is so stupid."

"I thought you weren't talking to me either," I said.

"I decided it was too immature," she said.

We made it to the Hansens and climbed the steps to their front porch.

"And your crazy aunt talks about doing spells and telling fortunes," said Rosemary T. "She's the biggest weirdo of all."

I could not believe my ears. I'd heard kids call other kids names, but I'd never heard a kid do that to a grown-up.

"Take that back, Rosemary T." I set Ralph down, and he pawed at his front door.

"No," Rosemary T. said. "She wears tons of bracelets and earrings and drives that smelly old car."

"I think her car is awesome," said Charlie.

"I think she's awesome," I said.

"That just makes you a big, weird weirdo too," said Rosemary T.

And right then and there I might have been pushed too far. "Rosema—," I started to say, but Mrs. Hansen opened her door.

"You caught him!"

Ralph barked and danced around like he was the happiest dog ever.

"If you like being home so much," Mrs. Hansen said, "why do you ever run away?"

Ralph wiggled his tail and raced inside.

"How about a piece of chocolate meringue pie as a reward?" Mrs. Hansen asked.

"I didn't really do anything," I said.

"Oh, you always do your fair share," said Mrs. Hansen. "You're welcome to come in too, Rosemary."

"No, thank you," said Rosemary T.

And that was a big *Phew*. It seemed like I was going to have to have a what's what after all, and

I did not want to have it in front of Charlie and Mrs. Hansen.

After we finished our reward, me and Charlie headed home.

"Really, really try to win the spelling bee, Cinderella," he said. "My table does not want to have a sparkly, pink, unicorn party."

"I'll try," I said. "I'm going to start studying again right when I get home."

"You should be studying every minute of every day," said Charlie, "like with me and basketball."

"I thought you played all the time just because you like it," I said.

"That's partly why, but also because I want to be the best." Charlie pretended he had a basketball and started dribbling right then and there. "So spell *basketball*."

"*B-a-s-k-e-t-b-a-l-l*."

"Good. Spell *dribbling*."

"*D-r-i-b-b-l-i-n-g*."

He jumped up in the air and pretended to shoot the basketball. "Spell *offense* and *defense*."

"*O-f-f-e-n-c-e. D-e-f-e-n-c-e*."

"It's *s-e*. Spell *forward*."

"*F-o-r-w-a-r-d*."

"Good. Spell *guard*."

"*G—*" I stopped. I knew there was something tricky about this word.

"Think about the lifeguard sign at the beach," he said.

"Oh yeah. *G-u-a-r-d*."

"Right. Spell *center*."

But luckily we got to my door, and I slipped inside. *"Phew!"* I said.

Aunt Flora and Tess looked up from a puzzle. "Why '*Phew*'?"

"Charlie was quizzing me on spelling, and I was getting tired," I said.

"You've had a long day," said Aunt Flora, "what with school and dance class and Ralph."

"Yep." Then I remembered something. "When you come to class tomorrow, can you bring something to give to the kids?"

"Like what?" she asked.

"I'm not sure," I said. "Rosemary T.'s dad brought in these paper penny roll things and that was really popular."

"I'm sure I can come up with something," said Aunt Flora.

I plunked down on the couch. "I guess I should start studying again."

"You don't sound too happy about that," said my aunt.

"I think I have some other things on my mind," I said.

"Like what?" asked Aunt Flora.

"Words," I said.

"Spelling bee words?"

"No, mean words," I said. "Rosemary T. called me names, and they're sort of blocking up my brain and making it hard to think about spelling."

"When I was a kid, we used to say 'Sticks and stones may break my bones, but names can never hurt me.'"

I thought hard about that for a minute. "I think names can hurt."

Aunt Flora looked like she was thinking hard for a minute too. "I think you're right. What were the words?"

"*Stupid* and *weird*," I said.

"*Weird*?" asked Aunt Flora. "I always thought *weird* was a good word."

"You did?"

"Sure," said my aunt. "I'd rather be called *weird*

than *ordinary* or *boring* any day. Weird people tend to be very interesting."

"Did you think that when you were a kid?" I asked.

"I don't remember," said Aunt Flora. "I also don't remember third grade being this complicated."

11

Golden
Strappy Sandals

Me and Erin were playing handball in the covered play court at recess when Hannah and Abby ran up to us all out of breath.

"Is your aunt really a witch?" asked Hannah.

"And does she really have a spooky, witch cat?" asked Abby.

"What are you talking about?" I said.

"Rosemary T. is telling everyone that your aunt is scary and weird," said Hannah. "So scary and weird that she might go home sick after recess just so she doesn't have to be here when your aunt visits."

I could not believe my ears at all.

"She says your aunt has a wart on her nose like a witch and does spells and fortunes," said Abby.

Right then and there I saw red-red-red! I knew for positive certain that I was pushed too far. "Where is Rosemary T.?"

"She's over by the basketball courts," said Hannah.

I marched out to find her, and Hannah ran ahead. Erin and Abby walked with me, but we didn't talk at all. I was too busy trying to figure out exactly what I wanted to say in my what's what with Rosemary T.

A bunch of kids were standing together under a basketball hoop, and the Rosemarys were right in the middle.

"Rosemary T.!" I yelled. "I need to talk to you!"

I walked up close to Rosemary T., and the rest of the third grade crowded in around us.

"You need to stop telling lies about my aunt this very minute!" I yelled right to her face.

Rosemary T. stared at me with big, open eyes and a big, open mouth.

Brrrrrrring! The end-of-recess bell rang, and kids

started running from everywhere to get in their lines. Everyone except me and Rosemary T.

"You have pushed too far," I said. "And I need—"

But Rosemary T. turned around and headed for our class line.

"I am not finished!" I yelled after her.

She ignored me and hurried to catch up with Rosemary W.

"Well, fine!" I yelled "Then meet me here at lunch."

I stomped over and got in at the end of the line and stomped right into class.

"Cinderella," Mr. Harrison said when we got inside.

My heart went down to my stomach. I thought for sure I was about to get in trouble for yelling and stomping and not getting into line right away.

"Why don't you tell us a little bit about your aunt while we wait for her?" is all he said.

"Sure!" I jumped up out of my seat, I was so relieved. "My aunt's name is Flora McGee. She's my mom's sister, and she works in a dentist office. She's taking care of me and Tess while our parents are away, and her cat is staying with us too." Then all of a sudden I had a huge *AHA!*

This was a vexylent chance to set the record straight.

"Her cat's name is Miss Purvis," I said. "She's mostly all white and is not at all spooky."

"Except she is pretty loud," said Charlie.

"I guess so," I said. "But it's just because she wants to go outside. Back to my aunt, she is not weird or scary at all. Everything about her is very, extremely regular and everyday."

"Her car isn't regular and everyday!" said Mr. Harrison.

"I guess not." I did a big sigh on account of all these interruptions. "But everything else about her is very normal. She's just a regular, old dental hygienist."

And right then the classroom door flew open and in came Aunt Flora. She had a crown on her head and was holding a wand in one hand and a big sack with a picture of a tooth on it in the other. "Hello, everyone!"

My heart went down to my stomach all over again. Aunt Flora was not helping me convince everyone that she was regular and normal at all.

"Cinderella calls me a dental hygienist, but I prefer the title Tooth Fairy." She did a little spin on her toes, and the golden strappy sandals she had on her feet sparkled a little bit.

I plunked down into my chair and put my head in my hands.

"Hey!" said Jack. "I know you. You clean my teeth."

I looked up. Jack didn't look too surprised by my aunt.

"Do I do a good job?" asked Aunt Flora.

"I don't know," said Jack.

"Do you have any cavities?" she asked.

"No," he said.

"Then I do," she said. "And so do you. You get a prize!" She reached into the bag she'd brought and handed Jack a little tube of toothpaste.

"Awesome!" he said. "Thanks!"

"You clean my teeth too," said Erin. "And you do a very good job."

"Thank you, Erin." Aunt Flora gave her a toothbrush.

"Mine too," said Charlie.

"Here you go, Charlie." Aunt Flora tossed him some floss.

"I wish you cleaned my teeth," said Trevor.

Aunt Flora smiled and sent a little tube of toothpaste his way. She waved her magic wand around a few times, and her bracelets jangled. "How often should you brush?"

"After every meal," the class called out.

Aunt Flora tossed out a handful of toothbrushes.

"Who here has lost a tooth?" she asked.

Hands went up everywhere, and little tubes of toothpastes and flosses went flying. Kids scrambled around picking them up like it was an egg hunt.

"I brush my dog's teeth," said Abby. "And you aren't scary at all, by the way."

Aunt Flora looked a little confused. "Thank you, I think." She reached deep in her bag and threw a package of little pink pills to her. "Those are disclosing tablets. After you brush and floss, chew one of them up. The dye turns any plaque left on your teeth pink so you can see where you need to brush better."

"Ooh," said Hannah. "I want some of those."

"Do you brush and floss?" Aunt Flora asked.

"Regularly," said Hannah.

"Bravo!" Aunt Flora threw some disclosing tablets to her too.

I looked over at Abby and Hannah. They smiled big at me, and I smiled big right back.

Aunt Flora kept asking questions and giving out teeth stuff. She was very, extremely fair; and by the end everyone had at least one thing.

"What a vexylent visitor!" said Mr. Harrison. "Not only did we learn what a dentist does, we also learned about taking care of our teeth."

"And it was fun too!" said Zachary, not so quiet after all.

A lot of kids agreed and I smiled, glad my aunt wasn't just plain regular and normal.

Aunt Flora got permission to stay for lunch, and

she was popular like you wouldn't believe. Our lunch table was jam-packed with kids wanting to sit by us.

After we ate, Erin and I gave Aunt Flora a tour of the school and introduced her to important people like the school secretary and the librarian. The only awshucksible thing about Aunt Flora being there was that I couldn't have my what's what with Rosemary T. Now that I'd started, I sort of wanted to finish.

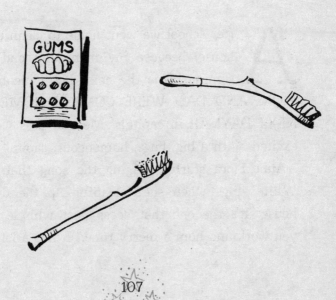

12

The What's What

After school we went home to clean up the house, because my mom and dad were coming home the next day. I mean, MY MOM AND DAD WERE COMING HOME THE NEXT DAY! All in capitals! Me and Tess were so excited, with a big, huge, humongous, capital *E*.

Aunt Flora started singing the song that Snow White sings when she's cleaning up the dwarfs' house. It's the one that goes: "Just whistle while you work and hum a merry tune." It has a lot more words; but we didn't know what they were, so we just sang that over and over. We also did some tap dancing and some jumping on furniture, and it turned out that cleaning up can actually be sort of fun.

Tess was in charge of picking toys up off the floor, and I was in charge of putting them away. Aunt Flora was in charge of vacuuming and dishes and anything else she thought of. All of a sudden, between the singing and tap dancing and cleaning, I heard the doorbell ringing and ringing, so I ran and opened it a crack.

"Finally!" yelled Rosemary T.

"Just a second," I said. "I'll go tell my aunt I'm going outside."

I shut the door and started to run to Tess's bedroom, where Aunt Flora was vacuuming; but Rosemary T. pushed open the front door just like it was her own. "Quit slamming the door in my face!"

"Shut the—," I started to say, but Miss Purvis was too fast. She dashed out the door. I ran outside, and Rosemary T. followed me.

For once in his life Charlie wasn't practicing basketball in his driveway, and it was the one time I really wished he was.

I watched Miss Purvis trot down the block. "See which way she goes," I ordered. "I have to let my aunt know what happened."

I ran back inside and yelled, "Aunt Flora! Miss Purvis escaped!"

Aunt Flora turned off the vacuum and came into the living room.

"What?" she asked.

"Miss Purvis escaped, and Charlie's not around to help me catch her," I said.

"I don't think you can really catch a cat," said Aunt Flora.

"Oh no." I crumbled down onto the floor and felt sick to my stomach. "There must be something I can do. Would food work?"

"You could try," said Aunt Flora.

We went into the kitchen and got a can of cat food.

"Here," said Aunt Flora, "these might help too." She slipped four of her bracelets on my arm, and I ran out the door.

"Now, are you finally going to talk to me?" asked Rosemary T.

"Now," I said, "I'm going to find Miss Purvis. Which way did she go?"

Rosemary T. pointed, and I headed down the block.

"Here, Miss Purvis! Here, kitty!" I waved the can of food around, and the bracelets jingled.

Rosemary T. followed after me. "Do you have to yell? It's so embarrassing."

That stopped me in my tracks. "I'm doing this because you let Miss Purvis out!"

"I don't mean just now," said Rosemary T. "I mean like today at recess."

"I had to yell to get you to stop talking." I started to walk again and jingled the bracelets.

"And now you're trying to be just like your aunt and wear tons of jewelry."

I started to tell her again that I was doing all this yelling and jingling because of her, but instead I just said, "I will take that as a compliment."

Rosemary T.'s mouth dropped open like I'd said something crazy. "Are you going to start wearing a crown and pretending to be the tooth fairy next?"

"Maybe," I said.

That stopped Rosemary T. in her tracks, but I kept

walking. I'd caught sight of Miss Purvis cleaning her paws a little ways down the block.

Rosemary T. caught up. "You're joking, right?"

"No," I said.

"But you're not weird like her," said Rosemary T. "You'll go back to normal when your mom and dad get home."

"I don't know about that," I said. "Weird people are interesting. I'd rather be weird than ordinary or boring any day."

"That's the dumbest thing I've ever heard." Rosemary T. looked very shocked.

"Rosemary T." I stopped and looked her right in the eyes. "I have been trying to ignore your meanness since the beginning of the year, but you have pushed me too far. Now it's time for me to tell you what's what."

"Is that another one of your childish, made-up words?" she asked.

"No," I said. "A what's what is a real, true thing."

"Well, I've never heard of it." She put her hands on her hips and looked right back at me. "Half of the time I can't understand a word you're saying."

"Well, I will speak slow and clear so you can." And right then I felt like I was giving a Table Book

Talk at school and not looking for Miss Purvis or having a what's what at all. "I feel like your Main Theme this year has been to be mean. To give a few examples of this, you keep talking all about your clubs in front of kids who aren't in them, and their feelings are getting hurt. You even made Kristy cry about the class party."

Something was tickling my ankles, but Rosemary T. just stood there and didn't say anything, so I kept talking. "You and Rosemary W. whisper all the time and make fun of people. You bug me about what I eat and some of the things I do too."

The tickling was still going on, but Rosemary T. and I were in the middle of a stare down. "You called me names and said really mean things about my aunt and Miss Purvis too." And then I realized the tickling was Miss Purvis, and I reached down and scooped her up. She rubbed her head under my chin and purred and purred. "And you can plainly see that this is not a spooky, black cat, just a very nice one." I started walking home before Miss Purvis could get tired of being held and start to do a Halloween yowl.

"Well, I think your Main Theme this year is to be a baby." Rosemary T. ran to catch up with me. "You don't have pierced ears and you always lose shoes and you hold your mom's hand! You even skip and sing with little kids."

Miss Purvis squirmed a little in my arms, but I rubbed her side and kept walking.

"In fact," said Rosemary T., "you're so weird and dumb and babyish that I don't want to be friends with you anymore!"

My feelings started hurting like the dickens, and I got tears in my eyes. There was no way I was going to let Rosemary T. see them, though. I buried my face in Miss Purvis's fur and walked faster.

"Did you hear me?" she said.

Of course I'd heard her, but I had a big lump of sad in my throat, and I could not get any words by it.

"I'm serious!" she said very loud.

And I believed her. We passed her house, but she kept walking with me.

"I am officially kicking you out of all my clubs! If we're not friends anymore, I don't want you in them!"

I thought about reminding her that I wasn't in all her clubs, but then I figured out that it didn't really matter. We made it to my front door, and Rosemary T. stood there with her hands on her hips waiting for me to say something.

The lump of sad in my throat was still there, but it was smaller and I could talk a little bit now. I couldn't think of anything to say, though, so I just said "Oh."

"Oh!" she shouted. "That's all you're going to say?"

My front door opened, and Aunt Flora stuck her head out. "Is everything all right?"

"Everything's fine," I said. "Our what's what got a little loud is all." I handed her Miss Purvis, and she nodded and shut the door.

Rosemary T. kept her hands on her hips and made mean stink eyes at me.

"We've been friends since we were babies," I said. "It would be weird to stop."

"It would not be weird," she said. "I'm never weird."

"Well, it might be awkward then."

"It will not. I just won't talk to you."

"I thought not talking was babyish," I said.

Rosemary's stink eyes got even stinkier. She made a big, huge, unicorn *harrumph* noise and huffed off down the block.

13

A Left-Behind Mary Jane

Since it was really, really raining the next morning, we got to go right up to our classrooms and not stand outside and get soaking wet. We could sit wherever we wanted to before the bell rang, so I sat next to Erin at her table and told her all about Rosemary T.

"I can't believe it; I just can't believe it," she said over and over and over.

"I know," I said. "I was very, extremely surprised at how my what's what turned out. I figured I'd tell

Rosemary T. how I was really feeling, and the air would clear and that would be that. Then she would go back to her old self, and things would be like they were before."

We both sat there all quiet, and I spun Aunt Flora's bracelets around and around my wrist.

"I like your bracelets," Erin finally said after lots of minutes.

"Thanks. My aunt said I could keep them forever as a reward for catching Miss Purvis."

Kristy and Olivia came in and sat down in their places at the table.

"Have you been studying a whole bunch, Cinderella?" asked Kristy.

"I've been trying," I said.

"Good," said Olivia. "Because we're all counting on you."

"Yeah," said Kristy. "I think the whole class is,

except the Rosemarys' table and Zachary."

"I want to win for sure," I said. "But if we happen to end up having a unicorn party, I don't think it will be too, too terrible."

Nobody said anything, so I said a little bit more. "Even if you don't believe in them, I think you could still have fun."

"It's more than just the party," said Olivia. "It's the Rosemarys."

"Yeah," said Kristy. "It's all their clubs and how they leave people out and call people names."

"I couldn't believe they called you a baby in the middle of the lunchroom," said Olivia. "You're one of their best friends."

"Not anymore," I said. "Rosemary T. told me she doesn't want to be friends, and she kicked me out of all of her clubs."

Kristy started patting me on the back to make me feel better. "I'll be your friend."

"Me too," said Olivia.

"Thanks," I said. And then I had an *AHA!* "Maybe we could start our own club."

"That's a great idea," said Erin.

"Who can be in it?" asked Olivia.

"Everyone," I said.

"What should we call it?" asked Kristy.

"I'm not sure," I said. "Oh, wait. I know: the More the Merrier Club."

I had been nervous about the whole spelling bee thing, but when we got to school that night I got even very, extremely, more nervous. There were eighteen chairs smooshed across the stage—six for fifth graders, six for fourth graders, and six for third graders—three from each class. Mrs. Bentley, our school secretary, called all the spellers to the stage and put us in seats alphabetically. I ended up between a fourth grader named Isaac Shaffer and Rosemary T., which was a little bit awshucksible. She gave me mean stink eyes like she'd been doing all day and sat on the very edge of her chair away from me.

"Welcome to the tenth annual Laurel Hill Elementary School Spelling Bee," our principal, Mrs. Shu, said. She started to go over the rules, and I started to pay very good attention and forgot all about Rosemary T.

"Rule number one, the contest shall be conducted in rounds. Each speller shall spell one word per round, and applause shall be held until the end of

the round." Mrs. Shu looked very serious at the audience. I did too, because I was looking to see if my mom and dad were there yet; but there were still two empty places next to Aunt Flora.

"Rule number two, spellers may ask to have a word repronounced, defined, or used in a sentence. Rule number three, spellers must pronounce the word, spell the word, and pronounce the word again. Rule number four, when it is your turn to spell, you shall stand at the microphone and spell slowly and clearly. And last, the most important rule of all, have fun!"

The audience started to clap and then stopped. They must not have known if that counted as the end of a round or not.

"Let's begin." Mrs. Shu nodded to Melissa Allen, a fourth-grade girl who walked up to the microphone.

"Miss Allen, your word is *agreeable*."

"*Agreeable*," said Melissa. "*A-g-r-e-e-a-b-l-e. Agreeable*."

Someone started to clap but then they remembered the rules and stopped.

A third grader from the other class went next.

"Mr. Bingham, your word is *already*."

A-l-r-e-a-d-y, I spelled to myself. But Fred Bingham spelled it *a-l-l-r-e-a-d-y*.

"I'm sorry, Mr. Bingham; that is incorrect," said Mrs. Shu. "Please join the audience."

Finally it was my turn. I walked up to the microphone a little shaky.

"Miss Smith, your word is *athlete*," said Mrs. Shu.

Since I'd made it through the *A*s in the dictionary, I knew this one for sure. "*Athlete. A-t-h-l-e-t-e. Athlete.*"

"Correct," said Mrs. Shu.

I smiled and looked out at the audience to where Aunt Flora and Tess were sitting. The two empty places next to them weren't empty anymore! They were full of my mom and dad! They smiled and waved, and I smiled big and went back to my seat.

"Miss Taylor," said Mrs. Shu, "your word is *believable*."

"Can you pronounce it again?" asked Rosemary T., so maybe she didn't hear it just right.

"*Believable*," said Mrs. Shu.

"*Believable*," said Rosemary T. "*B-e-l-i-e-v-a-b-l-e. Believable.*"

She spelled it right. *Alas.* And so did the next five people; and the round finished, and the audience finally got to clap.

I took the opportunity to give a little wave to my mom and dad, and my bracelets jingled.

"Be quiet!" hissed Rosemary T.

No one got out in round two, and no one started to clap by accident, so I guess we were all getting used to being at a spelling bee. Round three got a little harder. Emma from the other third-grade class mixed up where the *i* and *a* go in *alleviate*; and Leslie, who's also in that class, got mixed up about the *r* and the *e* in *mediocre*.

"Miss Smith," said Mrs. Shu, "your word is *herbicide.*"

For a minute I was a little stumped, but then I remembered about vegetarian dinosaurs eating plants and herbs. "*Herbicide. H-e-r-b-i-c-i-d-e. Herbicide.*"

"Correct," said Mrs. Shu. "Miss Taylor, your word is *scissors.*"

"Can you pronounce it again, please?" asked Rosemary T.

"*Scissors?*" Mrs. Shu pronounced it again, but this time like a question.

"Can you define it, please?" asked Rosemary T.

Mrs. Shu gave Rosemary T. a funny look, and I knew why. Everyone in that whole auditorium knew what scissors were. "A two-bladed cutting instrument."

"Can you—," said Rosemary T.

"No," said Mrs. Shu, "time to spell."

"*Scissors,*" said Rosemary T. "*S-c-i-s-.*" She stopped for a minute and started back up again. "*S-c-i-s-s-o-r-s. Scissors?*"

"Correct," said Mrs. Shu.

Next a fifth grader spelled *continuous* wrong, and a fourth grader spelled *renovate* wrong, and then that round was over and people clapped.

The fourth round had tons of hard *G* words. Isaac missed the word *ghoul*, and I got the word *guardian* and was sure I was going to miss it too. Then I remembered about lifeguards. *Phew!* Rosemary T. got *gymnasium,* and Mrs. Shu said it very slowly and told her she knew what it meant and that she should spell. And Rosemary T. did and got it right.

Round five was all full of words I had never even heard of like *appellate* and *bassoon*. I got *vernacular*; and thank goodness for figuring out where *vexylent* would live if it goes in the dictionary, because I got it right.

"Miss Taylor," said Mrs. Shu, "your word is *harangue*."

Rosemary T. stood there for a second and then she said, "Can you pronounce it again, please?"

"*Harangue*," Mrs. Shu said very slowly.

"Can you define it, please?" asked Rosemary T.

"A ranting speech," said Mrs. Shu.

"Can you use it in a sentence, please?" asked Rosemary T.

"Worried that someone might clap when they shouldn't, the principal decided to harangue the audience on spelling bee etiquette."

I didn't know about Rosemary T., but all this help from Mrs. Shu would not have helped me at all. The only thing that might have would have been eating chocolate meringue pie with Charlie and Mrs. Hansen and talking about the weird word that we were eating.

"*Harangue*," said Rosemary T. "*H-a-r-a-n-g. Harangue*."

"That is incorrect," said Mrs. Shu. "Please join the audience."

And when that round ended, I smiled the biggest ever and even clapped myself when it was time for applause. And maybe that wasn't too nice, but maybe it was okay. I've never had a not-friend before, so I'm not sure what exactly you do.

When round six started, I felt a little lonely up onstage. The two chairs on my right were empty and so was Rosemary T.'s on my left. I looked down to where Zachary was sitting, and he smiled at me. I gave him a thumbs-up, and he gave me a thumbs-up back; and I felt a little less alone.

The round was all full of *S*s. To give you a few examples, there was *saxophone* and *salmonella* and my word, *spaghetti*. I knew there was something tricky about my word, but I couldn't remember what it was. I also knew having a definition or a sentence wouldn't help. I knew what spaghetti was; I just didn't know how to spell it. All I could do was try my best. "*Spaghetti. S-p-a-g-e-t-t-i. Spaghetti.*"

"I'm sorry, Miss Smith, that is incorrect," said Mrs. Shu. "Please join the audience."

I gave Zachary another thumbs-up on my way to my seat, and he gave me another one back. Then I went and sat right on my dad's lap and grabbed hold of my mom's hand. I was sad, but not crying-about-it sad, because I was with my mom and dad and Aunt Flora and Tess. Then I noticed that I'd left behind one of my Mary Janes up onstage, tucked under my chair; and I did a great, big sigh. *Alas.*

We went out to get ice cream afterward; and the whole school seemed to have the same idea, because that place was packed.

"You may not have won," said Erin, "but you beat Rosemary T.!"

"Well done, Cinderella." Mr. Harrison squeezed past.

"I didn't know teachers went out for ice cream," said Erin.

"Me neither," I said.

Tons of third graders

kept squashing past us and saying hi.

Kristy and Olivia and Casey gave me hugs.

"Pretty vexylent," said Trevor.

"Congratulations, Cinderella." Rosemary T.'s mom squeezed by on her way to order ice cream.

"Yeah, good job, Cinderella," said Rosemary T.'s oldest sister.

"Thank you," I said. "And good job to you too, Rosemary T."

Rosemary T. didn't say anything.

"Where are your manners, Rosemary?" said her middle sister.

Rosemary T. gave me mean stink eyes.

"Don't be so immature, Rosemary," said her oldest sister.

Rosemary T. clamped her lips together and didn't say a word.

"I guess we have to apologize for our *baaaaaby* sister." Rosemary T.'s oldest sister flipped her hair and headed to the counter where their mom was.

"How embarrassing." Rosemary T.'s middle sister rolled her eyes and followed.

"*Harangue* is a very hard word." I felt sort of bad for Rosemary T. all of a sudden.

Rosemary T. looked like maybe she was going to

say something; but her mom called her over to the counter, and she went to get her ice cream.

Zachary started to inch past, but all the third graders stopped him. We patted him on the back and yelled "Hurray" and gave him high fives and tens.

Abby and Hannah squished into the group too. "You did awesome too, Cinderella!"

Charlie pushed through a bunch of people to stand next to us. He was holding his basketball in one hand and had the other hand behind his back. "Good job! If you had gotten out on *athlete*, I would have been really mad."

"Charlie!" Charlie's mom called from somewhere in the ice cream place. "Here's your cone!"

"Gotta go!" said Charlie. "Oh yeah, here." He pulled his hand from behind his back and handed me my Mary Jane.

"Oh, I forgot about that," I said. "Thanks."

"No problemo." Charlie pushed away.

My dad appeared out of nowhere holding Tess on his shoulders. "About ready to go?"

"Yep," I said. "Can Erin spend the night?"

"It works for me," said my dad. "Let's go check with the moms."

We said good-bye to everyone, and I grabbed on to my dad's belt and Erin grabbed on to my hood. We chug-a-chugged right behind him like we were a train, and that was a way easier way to get around and out of that jammed-packed place, FYI.

14

More of Everything

On Saturday morning we went out for breakfast, and when we got home we saw a sort of strange sight. Loud Charlie and quiet Zachary were standing in Charlie's driveway, wearing all blue. Erin and I ran over to see what this was all about.

"I didn't know you were Cub Scouts," I said when I got closer and saw the uniforms.

"Zachary's been one for a while," said Charlie, "but I'm just starting."

"I showed Charlie how to make a pinewood derby car," said Zachary. "Now Charlie's going to teach me some basketball moves."

"That sounds like a good trade," I said. "Congratulations on the spelling bee again."

"Thanks." Zachary looked down at his feet.

"Did you pick a party theme?" asked Erin.

Zachary looked up, and his cheeks were a little red. "Not yet. My mom told me I had to decide by the time she picks me up, and that's in only two hours."

"What are you trying to choose from?" asked Erin.

"I can't decide yet, still." Zachary looked very worried.

"Do you want some help?" I asked.

Zachary's worried look went away a little bit. "Yes!"

"How about basketball," said Charlie.

"Or animals," said Erin.

"Or Cub Scouts," said Charlie.

"Or tap dancing," said Erin.

Zachary's worried look got even worried-er than before.

"I don't think this is helping," I said.

"There are a lot of good ideas," said Erin.

"Too many good ideas," said Zachary.

Then all of a sudden I had an *AHA!*, and it was so good that I said it out loud by accident.

"What?" asked Erin and Charlie and Zachary all at the same time.

"Come over to my house, and I'll tell you all about it."

So everybody followed me home, and they liked my idea and we got to work.

On Monday, right after lunch, Mr. Harrison said it was time for the festivities to begin.

The first thing we did was decorate. Me and Erin and Zachary and Charlie had emailed the whole class and asked them to bring in a picture of one of their favorite things. I brought a picture of my last dance recital, where I'm wearing my shiny, red tap shoes with a fancy bow. Erin brought a picture of Anna and Julia and me from her mom's wedding. Zachary brought a picture of his hamster, Fred, and Charlie brought a basketball picture, of course. Mr. Harrison brought a picture of an Opel GT that he printed off the computer.

People started taping their pictures up, and everywhere you looked there were animals and sports teams and UFOs and about everything else you could imagine.

Pretty soon the room-parents started coming in with treats. To give you a few examples, my mom brought Rice Krispies Treats, and Erin's mom brought popcorn, and Zachary's mom brought string cheese, and Charlie's mom brought brownies. There were also pretzels and cupcakes and orange slices and cookies and lots of different things to drink.

"I think we have enough to feed an army," said Mr. Harrison.

And I think he was right. I have never seen so much food at a class party before. Or so many decorations either. While the room-parents set up the food, the class drew pictures of more of their favorite things and hung those up too.

"This is a great idea, Zachary," Christopher called from across the room.

"It was really Cinderella's idea," Zachary called back.

"No way," I said. "I just got the ball rolling. It was yours and mine and Erin's and Charlie's too!"

"I like it 'cause it's not too girly," said Jack.

"And it's not too boyly either," said Olivia.

"Also," said Logan, "there's plenty of levity."

Kristy walked over to the wall and taped up a picture of a horse.

"That is a vexylent picture!" said Hannah.

I was so surprised to hear Hannah use my word that my mouth popped wide-open.

"Hannah!" The Rosemarys spun around in their chairs and stared hard at her.

Hannah covered her mouth with her hand for a second, and her eyes opened wide. Then she put her hand back down. "It *is* vexylent," she said. "Kristy, will you teach me how to draw a horse and help me add a horn to make it a unicorn?"

"Sure!" said Kristy. "Come over to our table."

"Me too!" said Abby.

"Class, please take a seat," said Mr. Harrison.

We all just took a seat wherever we were.

"I'm very proud of you," he said. "You all worked hard and did a fine job improving your spelling skills. Bravo!" He started clapping, and the room-parents joined in and then the rest of us did too.

"Zachary, Rosemary T., and Cinderella, please come up front."

We all three went up to his desk, and he shook our hands and gave us each a ribbon.

One of the room-parents wanted to take our picture, so we all stood still and smiled. After the flash I looked down and saw I was only wearing socks, but Rosemary T. didn't tattle or anything.

Just then the door opened, and Mrs. Kirk stuck her head in. "Sorry to interrupt."

"That's okay," said me and Zachary and Rosemary T. and Mr. Harrison at the same time. Then we all four started laughing.

"We were just about to start celebrating last week's spelling successes," said Mr. Harrison.

And right then and there I had another great, big *AHA!* I whispered it to Zachary, and he pulled on Mr. Harrison's sleeve and said, "Would it be okay if we invited Mrs. Kirk's class to come too?"

"Oh, I don't know . . . ," said Mrs. Kirk.

"That's a grand idea," said Mr. Harrison. "We have plenty to share."

We all had friends in the other third-grade class, so a lot of kids agreed.

"If you did come," I said, "it would go right with our party's Main Theme."

"What is your party's Main Theme?" she asked.

"It's a More of Everything party," said Zachary. "More party ideas and more decorations and more food and more people—if your class comes, that is."

"Please do come," said Mr. Harrison.

"Because, you know," I said, "the more the merrier."

Catch a sneak peek!

Cinderella Smith

The Super Secret Mystery

After a class trip to the zoo, Cinderella can't wait to start her animal report. But when all the books she needs suddenly go missing from the library, a strange note with a clue appears on Cinderella's desk. Will she be able to solve this super secret mystery before her report is due?

1

Ladybug Boots

"Do you ever think about what you want to be when you grow up?" I asked my best friend, Erin.

"All the time," she said. "Right now I think I might want to be a scientist like my stepdad. What do you want to be?"

"I'm not sure," I said. "But I definitely don't want to be a school bus driver."

"Why not?"

"Because being on school buses makes me a little sick to my stomach."

"Let's change seats," said Erin. "Sometimes being

by the window helps. Also, look out, not in."

I rubbed the fog off the window with my hand and looked outside. The sky was all full of dribbly-spit, which is not good field trip weather. *Alas.*

"Do you feel better?" Erin asked after a few minutes.

"What's wrong?" Charlie had poked his head over from the seat behind us.

"Cinderella feels a little sick," said Erin.

"Is she going to throw up?" he asked.

"No," I said.

"Maybe we should open the window, just in case." Charlie reached over and tried to push it up.

"What's going on?" asked Jack, Charlie's seatmate.

"Nothing," I said.

"Cinderella's feeling sick," said Charlie.

"We need a barf bag at the back of the bus!" yelled Jack. "Cinderella's going to blow!"

"I am not," I said.

"Cinderella, that's disgusting." Rosemary T. leaned across the aisle. And FYI, Rosemary T. and I used to be friends, but we're not so much anymore.

"Don't get too close!" Rosemary W., Rosemary T.'s best friend, pulled her back into her seat.

"Is everything okay back there?" our teacher, Mr.

Harrison, called from up front.

"Everything's fine," I called back.

"Cinderella's about to throw up!" Rosemary T. yelled at the same time.

"I am not!" I said.

"She is not!" said Erin.

"It looks like she is," said Rosemary W.

"I'm *fine*," I said to the Rosemarys.

"Are you sure?" Mr. Harrison walked to the back of the bus, even though you're not supposed to get out of your seat when the bus is moving. He looked at me very concerned.

"I'm positive," I said. "I felt a little sick for a minute, but now I'm just fine and dandy." With everyone making such a big deal of it, I was for sure going to be fine and dandy too.

"Okay, but let me know if you start to feel bad again." Mr. Harrison walked back up to the front. "We'll be at the zoo in about five minutes."

"I can't wait to get there," I said to Erin. "And not because I was feeling sick. Just because it's one of the best places ever."

"I know," said Erin. "I love the zoo, especially the penguins."

"Me too," I said. "And the meerkats and the red

3

pandas and the Komodo dragons."

"And everything in the Day House." Zachary leaned over the back of his seat in front of us.

"You shouldn't get too close to Cinderella," said Rosemary T. "She's probably highly contagious."

I did a big, huge sigh, and Erin and I rolled our eyes at each other.

"I'm not scared of her," said Zachary.

I gave him a thumbs-up, and he gave me one back and bumped my knuckles with his.

"Hey," I said, "that's vexylent! A thumbs-up-bump!"

"Don't you dare start making up words again," said Rosemary T.

I like to make up words and try to get them in the dictionary. A couple weeks ago I made up *vexylent*, which means "very, extremely excellent." I guess she thought *thumbs-up-bump* was a new one I was trying out.

"Thumbs-up-bump! Thumbs-up-bump!" Erin and Zachary and I chanted and bumped each other at the same time.

"Now you're really getting germy, Zachary," said Rosemary T. "Be sure to use some hand sanitizer."

"I am not," said Zachary.

"Neither am I." Charlie stuck his head right between me and Erin and patted me on the head.

"Cut it out, Charlie," I said.

Then the bus stopped and the door hissed open and a zoo person jumped on. She did a *clap, clap, clap-clap-clap*, and we did one back and then got quiet.

"Wow." She sounded pretty impressed. I guess not everyone knows about clapping back and then listening. "Welcome to Woodland Park Zoo. Are you Mr. Harrison's third-grade class?"

"Yes!" we all said.

"Here to learn about endangered animals?"

"Yes," only a few of us said. I guess some kids forgot why we were here.

"Okay," said the zoo person. "Follow me, and we'll go see some animals!"

"Yay!" everyone yelled, and we filed off the bus.

"Are you the last one?" the zoo person asked.

"Yep," I said. "Sorry if you had to wait. I took my boots off on the ride over, and it took me a little while to get them back on."

She looked down at my feet. "Those are great boots."

I looked down at my rain boots too. "Thank you. I picked bright red with black polka dots so they would be harder to lose."

"You could put your name on them too. That's what I do with my hats." She took her hat off and showed me the inside, where it said "Robin Chrispin."

"I always put my name and address on the bottoms." I grabbed on to Erin and kicked my leg out in front to show her.

"Cinderella?" Robin read the name off the bottom of my boot.

"It's just my nickname," I said.

"Because she loses shoes a lot," said Erin.

"But they get returned to me this way," I said.

"Glad to hear it," said Robin. "Follow me, everyone."

We walked along a curvy path, and I knew we

were heading to the Tropical Rain Forest area. I was very, extremely familiar with the zoo because my whole family likes it here. Robin stopped in front of a big glass window.

"I don't see anything," said Rosemary T.

"It's the gorilla exhibit," I said.

"I know *that*," she said. "But where are they?"

"They're probably hiding from you," said Jack.

"Harrumph!" said Rosemary T.

Just then the gorillas came out. We watched them wander around their exhibit, picking up lettuce and other vegetables that were scattered all over.

"Can anyone tell me why gorillas are endangered?" asked Robin.

"Mainly because of limited resources," said Logan.

"What's that mean?" asked Zachary.

"It means they're running out of the things they need to survive," said Logan. "Like places to live and food to eat."

"I'm impressed," said Robin. "You know your stuff."

"I'm doing my endangered species report on gorillas, and I already have some notes," said Logan.

I was impressed too. I hadn't thought much about the report yet, but maybe I should start.

"Let's move on."

We followed Robin to the next exhibit.

"The animal that lives here is pretty shy, so keep your voices low," said Robin.

"I just saw some leaves move!" yelled Zachary.

Everyone shushed him.

A big, beautiful jaguar pushed through some bushes. It stood on the other side of the glass looking right at me. Everyone crowded around and *ooh*ed and *aah*ed very quietly.

"Move, Cinderella," hissed Rosemary T. "I want to see better."

I stepped back and crashed into Rosemary W.

"Ooh!" Rosemary W. yelled, and the jaguar moved away from the glass.

"Good job, Rosemary W.," said Charlie.

"Let's be quiet, and he'll come back," said Robin. "Why do you think jaguars are endangered?"

"Because of their beautiful fur." Rosemary W. pushed right up next to Rosemary T.

"Yes," said Robin. "Any other reasons?"

"Also their limited resources," said Rosemary T.

"Exactly," said Robin. "They're hunted for their fur and are losing their habitat. Many other animals are too, like gorillas, as we discussed before."

We went into the Tropical Rain Forest building.

It was warm and wet, and people's glasses got all fogged up.

"Now that we're inside we can spread out and explore at our own pace," said Robin.

"Grab a buddy and take notes in preparation for your reports," said Mr. Harrison.

Erin grabbed me and I grabbed her, and we headed off.

"What lives here?" Erin asked the Rosemarys, who were standing in front of a big glass window.

"Nothing," said Rosemary T.

"We've been here for hours," said Rosemary W. "It's empty."

"We've only been in the building for a few minutes." I sat down in front of the exhibit.

"You probably weren't patient enough." Erin walked over to the sign, and the Rosemarys huffed away.

"It says a highly endangered ocelot lives here." Erin kept reading, and I took a ton of notes.

"I think I see it!" From where I was sitting, I could

see a tail hanging down from a tall branch.

"It was really blending in up there." Erin sat down next to me, and we started sketching.

"Hey, maybe that's what happened to my missing leopard-print flat," I said. "Maybe it's camouflaged somewhere."

"We'll go on a search next time I'm over," said Erin.

"And we won't look inside this time," I said. "We'll look all over the garden and places outside."

The next exhibit was full of hissing cockroaches, which were not endangered so we didn't spend much time with them.

"We're taking a poll." Christopher and Trevor were standing in front of a snake exhibit. "Would you rather trip over a boa constrictor or a bushmaster?"

"Neither." Erin walked over to the next cage, where two toucans were sitting on a branch.

"Hmm." I thought for a minute. "I'd rather trip on a boa constrictor. At least I'd have a chance of staying alive with that guy."

"Excellent answer," said Christopher. "The bushmaster's venom would be the end of you, but you might be able to elude the constrictor."

"*Phew!*" I hurried to catch up to Erin.

We tried to sketch golden lion tamarin monkeys,

but they were jumping around their cage too fast.

"They're cute," said Erin.

"But frustrating," I said.

The poison dart frogs next door were much easier to draw.

"I wish I could have one of these for a pet," said Charlie.

"But you could never play with it," I said.

"It says they lose their poison in captivity," he said.

Read about Blackberry Lane's spunky and lovable third-grader,

Cinderella Smith

HARPER

An Imprint of HarperCollinsPublishers

www.harpercollinschildrens.com